THE RIDDLE OF
THE FROZEN FLAME

THE RIDDLE OF THE FROZEN FLAME

BY MARY E. AND THOMAS W. HANSHEW

MYSTERY CLASSICS

BOOK INFORMATION

Published by Wildside Press, LLC
www.wildsidebooks.com

CHAPTER

SUBTITLE

CHAPTER I

THE LAW

Mr. Maverick Narkom, Superintendent of Scotland Yard, sat before the litter of papers upon his desk. His brow was puckered, his fat face red with anxiety, and there was about him the air of one who has reached the end of his tether.

He faced the man opposite, and fairly ground his teeth upon his lower lip.

"Dash it, Cleek!" he said for the thirty-third time, "I don't know what to make of it, I don't, indeed! The thing's at a deadlock. Hammond reports to me this morning that another bank in Hendon—a little one-horse affair—has been broken into. That makes the third this week, and as usual every piece of gold is gone. Not a bank note touched, not a bond even fingered. And the thief—or thieves—made as clean a get-away as you ever laid your eyes on! I tell you, man, it's enough to send an average person daft! The whole of Scotland Yard's been on the thing, and we haven't traced 'em yet! What do you make of it, old chap?"

"As pretty a kettle of fish as I ever came across," responded Cleek, with an enigmatic smile. "And I can't help having a sneaking admiration for the person who's engineering the whole thing. How he must laugh at the state of the old Yard, with never a clue to settle down upon, never a thread to pick up and unravel! All of which is unbusinesslike of me, I've no doubt. But, cheer up, man, I've a piece of news which ought to help matters on a bit. Just came from the War Office, you know."

Mr. Narkom mopped his forehead eagerly. The action was one which Cleek knew showed that every nerve was tense.

"Well, out with it, old chap! Anything to cast some light on the inexplicable thing. What did you learn at the War Office?"

"A good many things—after I had unravelled several hundred yards of red tape to get at 'em," said Cleek, still smiling. "Chief among them was this: Much English gold has been discovered in Belgium, Mr. Narkom, in connection with several big electrical firms engaged upon work out there. The Secret Service wired over that fact, and I got it first hand. Now it strikes me there must be some connection between the two things. These bank robberies point in one direction, and that is, that the gold is not for use in this country. Now let's hear the full account of this latest outrage. I'm all ears, as the donkey said to the ostrich. Fire away."

Mr. Narkom "fired away" forthwith. He was a bland, round little man, rather too fat for one's conceptions of what a policeman ought to be, yet with that lightness of foot that so many stout people seem to possess.

Cleek presented a keen contrast to him. His broad-shouldered, well-groomed person would have adorned any company. His head was well-set upon his neck, and his features at this moment were small and inclined to be aquiline. He had closely set ears that lay well back against his head, and his hands were slim and exceedingly well-kept. Of his age—well that, like himself, was an enigma. To-day he might have been anything between thirty-five and forty—to-morrow probably he would be looking nineteen. That was part of the peculiar birthright of the man, that and a mobility of feature which enabled him to alter his face completely in the passing of a second, a gift which at least one notorious criminal of history also possessed.

He sat now, playing with the silver-topped cane between his knees, his head slightly to one side, his whole manner one of polite and tolerant interest. But Mr. Narkom knew that this same manner marked an intensity of concentration which was positively unique. Without more ado he plunged into the details of his story.

"It happened in this wise, Cleek," he said, tapping his fountain-pen against his blotter until little spouts of ink fell out like jet beads. "This is at least the ninth case of the kind we've had reported to us within the space of the last fortnight. The first robbery was at a tiny branch bank in Purley, and the bag amounted to a matter of a couple of hundred or so sovereigns; the second was at Peckham—on the outskirts, you understand; the third at Harrow; the fourth somewhere near Forest Hill, and the fifth in Croydon. Other places on the South East side of London have come in for their share, too, as for instance Anerley and Sutton. This last affair took place at Hendon, during the evening of Saturday last—the sixteenth, wasn't it? No one observed anything untoward in the least, that is except one witness who relates how he saw a motor car standing outside the bank's premises at half past nine at night. He gave no thought to this, as he probably imagined, if he thought of the coincidence at all, that the manager had called there for something he had forgotten in his office."

"And where, then, does the manager live, if not over the bank itself?" put in Cleek at this juncture.

"With his wife and family, in a house some distance away. A couple of old bank people—a porter and his wife who are both thoroughly trustworthy in every way, so Mr. Barker tells me act as caretakers. But they positively assert that they heard no one in the place that night, and no untoward happening occurred to their knowledge."

"And yet the bank was broken into, and the gold taken," supplemented Cleek quietly. "And what then, Mr. Narkom? How was the deed done?"

"Oh, the usual methods. The skeleton keys of a master crook obviously opened the door to the premises themselves, and soup was used to crack the safe. Everything was left perfectly neat and tidy and only the bags of gold—amounting to seven hundred and fifty pounds— were gone. And not a trace of a clue to give one a notion of who did the confounded thing, or where they came from!"

"Hmm. Any finger-prints?"

Mr. Narkom shook his head.

"None. The thief or thieves used rubber gloves to handle the thing. And that was the only leg given us to stand upon, so to speak. For rubber gloves, when they are new, particularly, possess a very strong smell, and this still clung to the door-knob of the safe, and to several objects near it. That was how we deduced the rubber-glove theory of no finger-prints at all, Cleek."

"And a very worthy deduction too, my friend," responded that gentleman, with something of tolerance in his smile. "And so you have absolutely nothing to go by. Poor Mr. Narkom! The path of Law and Justice is by no means an easy one to tread, is it? Of course you can count upon me to help you in every way. That goes without saying. But I can't help thinking that this news from the War Office with regard to English gold in Belgium has something to do with these bank robberies, my friend. The two things seem to hang together in my mind, and a dollar to a ducat that in the long run they identify themselves thus. … Hello! Who's that?" as a tap sounded at the door. "I'll be off if you're expecting visitors. I want to look into this thing a little closer. Some time or other the thieves are bound to leave a clue behind. Success breeds carelessness, you know, and if they think that Scotland Yard is giving the business up as a bad job, they won't be so deuced particular as to clearing up afterward. We'll unravel the thing between us, never fear."

"I wish I could think so, old chap!" said Mr. Narkom, a trifle gloomily, as he called "Come in!" The door opened to admit Petrie, very straight and business-like. "But you're no end of a help. It does me good just to see you. What is it, Petrie?"

"A gentleman to see you, sir," responded the constable in crisp tones. "A gentleman by name of Merriton, Sir Nigel Merriton he said his name was. Bit of a toff I should say by the look of 'im. And wants to see you partikler. He mentioned Mr. Cleek's name, sir, but I told 'im he wasn't in at the moment. Shall I show him up?"

"Quite right, Petrie," laughed Cleek, in recognition of this act of one of the Yard's subordinates; for everyone was to do everything in his power to shield Cleek's identity. "I'll stay if you don't mind, Mr. Narkom. I happen to know something of this Merriton. A fine upstanding young man, who, once upon a time was very great friends with Miss Lorne. That was in the old Hawksley days. Chap's lately come into his inheritance, I believe. Uncle disappeared some five or six years ago and legal time being up, young Merriton has come over to claim his own. The thing made a newspaper story for a week when it happened, but they never found any trace of the old man. And now the young one is over here, bearing the title, and I suppose living as master of the Towers—spooklike spot that it is! Needn't say who I am, old chap, until I hear a bit. I'll just shift over there by the window and read the news, if you don't mind."

"Right you are." Mr. Narkom struggled into his coat—which he generally disposed of during private office hours. Then he gave the order for the gentleman to be shown in and Petrie disappeared forthwith.

But during the time which intervened before Merriton's arrival, Cleek did a little "altering" in face and general get-up, and when he *did* appear certainly no one would have recognized the aristocratic looking individual of a moment or two before, in an ordinary-appearing, stoop-shouldered, rather racy-looking tout.

"Ready," said Cleek at last, and Mr. Narkom touched the bell upon his table. Immediately the door opened and Petrie appeared followed closely by young Sir Nigel Merriton, whose clean-cut face was grim and whose mouth was set forbiddingly.

And in this fashion was Cleek introduced to the chief character of a case which was to prove one of the strangest of his whole career. There was nothing about Sir Nigel, a well-dressed man about town, to indicate that he was to be the centre of an extraordinary drama, yet such was to be the case.

He was obviously perturbed, but those who sought Mr. Narkom's counsel were frequently agitated; for no one can be even remotely connected with crime in one form or another without showing excitement to a greater or lesser degree. And so his manner by no means set Sir Nigel apart from many another visitor to the Superintendent's sanctum.

Mr. Narkom's cordial nod brought from the young man a demand to see "Mr. Cleek," of whom he had heard such wonderful tales. Mr. Narkom, with one eye on that very gentleman's back, announced gravely that Cleek was absent on a government case, and asked what he could do. He waved a hand in Cleek's direction and said that here was one of his men who would doubtless be able to help Sir Nigel in any difficulty he might happen to be in at the moment.

Now, as Sir Nigel's story was a long one, and as the young man was too agitated to tell it altogether coherently, we will go back for a certain space of time, and tell the very remarkable story, the details of which were told to Mr. Narkom and his nameless associate in the Superintendent's office, and which was to involve Cleek of Scotland Yard in a case which was later to receive the title of the Riddle of the Frozen Flame.

Much that he told them of his family history was already known to Cleek, whose uncanny knowledge of men and affairs was a by-word, but as that part of the story itself was not without romance, it must be told too, and to do so takes the reader back to a few months before his present visit to the precincts of the Law, when Sir Nigel Merriton returned to England after twelve years of army life in India. A few days he had spent in London, renewing acquaintances, revisiting places he knew—to find them wonderfully little changed—and then had journeyed to Merriton Towers, the place which was to be his, due to the extraordinary disappearance of his uncle—a disappearance which was yet to be explained.

Ill luck had often seemed to dog the footsteps of his house and even his journey home was not without a mishap; nothing serious, as things turned out, but still something that might have been vastly so. His train was in a wreck, rather a nasty one, but Nigel himself had come out unscathed, and much to be congratulated, he thought, since through that wreck he has become acquainted with what he firmly believed to be the most beautiful girl in the world. Better yet, he had learned that she was a neighbour of his at Merriton Towers. That fact helped him through what he felt was going to be somewhat of an ordeal—his entrance into the gloomy and ghost-ridden old house of his inheritance.

CHAPTER II
THE FROZEN FLAMES

Merriton Towers had been called the loneliest spot in England by many of the tourists who chanced to visit the Fen district, and it was no misnomer. Nigel, having seen it some thirteen years before, found that his memory had dimmed the true vision of the place considerably; that where he had builded romance, romance was not. Where he had softened harsh outlines, and peopled dark corridors with his own fancies, those same outlines had taken on a grimness that he could hardly believe possible, and the long, dark corridors of his mind's vision were longer and darker and lonelier than he had ever imagined any spot could be.

It was a handsome place, no doubt, in its gaunt, gray, prisonlike way. And, too, it had a moat and a miniature portcullis that rather tickled his boyish fancy. The furnishings, however, had an appalling grimness that took the very heart out of one. Chairs which seemed to have grown in their places for centuries crowded the corners of hallway and stairs like gigantic nightmares of their original prototypes. Monstrous curtains of red brocade, grown purple with the years, seemed to hang from every window and door crowding out the light and air. The carpets were thick and dark and had lost all sign of pattern in the dull gloom of the centuries.

It was, in fact, a house that would create ghosts. The atmosphere was alive with that strange sensation of disembodied spirits which some very old houses seem to possess. Narrow, slit-like windows in perfect keeping with the architecture and the needs of the period in which it was built—if not with modern ideas of hygiene and health—kept the rooms dark and musty. When Nigel first entered the place through the great front door thrown open by the solemn-faced butler, who he learned had been kept on from his uncle's time, he felt as though he were entering his own tomb. When the door shut he shuddered as the light and sunshine vanished.

The first night he hardly slept a wink. His bed was a huge four-poster, girt about with plush hangings like over-ripe plums, that shut him in as though he were in some monstrous Victorian trinket box. A post creaked at every turn he made in its downy softnesses, and being used to the light, camp-like furniture of an Indian bungalow he got up, took an eiderdown with him, and spent the rest of the hours upon a sofa drawn up beside an open window.

"That people could live in such places!" he told himself, over and over again. "No wonder my poor old uncle disappeared! Any self-respecting Christian would. There'll be some slight alterations made in Merriton Towers before I'm many days older, you can bet your life on that. Old great-grandmother four-poster takes her *congé* to-morrow morning. If I must live here I'll sleep anyhow."

He settled himself back against the hard, horsehair sofa, and pulled up the blind. The room was instantly filled with gray and lavender shadows, while without the Fens stretched out in unbroken lines as though all the rest of the world were made up of nothing else. Lonely? Merriton had known the loneliness of Indian nights, far away from any signs of civilization: the loneliness of the jungle when the air was so still that the least sound was like the dropping of a bomb; the strange mystical loneliness which comes to the only white man in a town of natives. But all these were as nothing as compared to this. He could imagine a chap committing suicide living in such a house. Sir Joseph Merriton had disappeared five years before—and no wonder!

Merriton lay with his eyes upon the window, smoking a cigarette, and surveyed the outlook before him with despairing eyes. What a future for a chap in his early thirties to face! Not a sign of habitation anywhere, not a vestige of it, save at the far edge of the Fens where a clump of trees and thick shrubs told him that behind lay Withersby Hall. This, intuition told him, was the home of Antoinette Brellier, the girl of the train, of the wreck, and now of his dreams. Then his thoughts turned to her. Gad! to bring a frail, delicate little butterfly to a place like this was like trying to imprison a ray of sunshine in a leaden box! …

His eyes, rivetted upon where the clump of trees stood out against the semi-darkness of the approaching dawn, saw of a sudden a light prick out like a tiny flame, low down upon the very edge of the Fens. One light, two, three, and then a very host of them flashed out, as though some unseen hand had torn the heavens down and strewn their jewels broadcast over the marshes. Instinctively he got to his feet. What on earth—? But even as his lips formed the unspoken exclamation came yet another light to join the others dancing and twinkling and flickering out there across the gloomy marshlands.

What the dickens was it, anyhow? A sort of unearthly fireworks display, or some new explosive experiment? The dancing flames got into his eyes like bits of lighted thistledown blown here, there, and everywhere.

Merriton got to his feet and threw open another window bottom with a good deal of effort, for the sashes were old and stiff. Then, clad only in his silk pyjamas, and with the cigarette charring itself to a tiny column of gray ash in one hand, he leaned far out over the sill and watched those twinkling, dancing, maddening little star-flames, with the eyes of amazed astonishment.

In a moment sleep had gone from his eyelids and he felt thoroughly awake. Dashed if he wouldn't throw on a few clothes and investigate. The thing was so strange, so incredible! He knew, well enough, from Borkins's (the venerable butler) description earlier in the evening, that that part of the marshes was uninhabited. Too low for stars the things were, for they hung on the edges of the marsh grass like tiny lanterns swung there by fairy hands. In such a house, in such a room, with the shadow of that old four-poster winding its long fingers over him, Merriton began to perspire. It was so devilish uncanny! He was a brave enough man in human matters, but somehow these flames out there in the uninhabited stretch of the marshes were surely caused by no human agency. Go and investigate he would, this very minute! He drew in his head and brought the window down with a bang that went sounding through the gaunt, deserted old house.

Hastily he began to dress, and even as he struggled into a pair of tweed trousers came the sound of a soft knock upon his door, and he whipped round as though he had been shot, his nerves all a-jingle from the very atmosphere of the place.

"And who the devil are you?" he snapped out in an angry voice, all the more angry since he was conscious of a slight trembling of the knees. The door swung open a trifle and the pale face of Borkins appeared around it. His eyes were wide with fright, his mouth hung open.

"Sir Nigel, sir. I 'eard a dreadful noise—like a pistol shot it was, comin' from this room! Anythink the matter, sir?"

"Nothing, you ass!" broke out Merriton, fretfully, as the butler began to show other parts of his anatomy round the corner of the door. "Come in, or go out, which ever you please. But for the Lord's sake, do one or the other! There's a beastly draught. The noise you heard was that window which possibly hasn't been opened for a century or two, groaning in pain at being forced into action again! Can't sleep in this beastly room—haven't closed my eyes yet—and when I did get out of that Victorian atrocity over there and take to the sofa by the window, why, the first thing I saw were those flames flickering out across the horizon like signal-fires, or *something*! I've been watching them for the past twenty minutes and they've got on my nerves. I'm goin' out to investigate."

Borkins gave a little exclamation of alarm and put one trembling hand over his face. Merriton suddenly registered the fact as being a symptom of the state of nerves which Merriton Towers was likely to reduce one. Then Borkins shambled across the room and laid a timid hand upon Merriton's arm.

"For Gawd's sake sir—*don't!*" he murmured in a shaken voice. "Those lights, sir—if you knew the story! If you values your life at any price at all don't go out, sir, and investigate them. *Don't!* You're a dead man in the morning if you do."

"What's that?" Merriton swung round and looked into the weak, rather watery, blue eyes of his butler. "What the devil do you mean, Borkins, talkin' a lot of rot? What *are* those flames, anyway? And why in heaven's name shouldn't I go out and investigate 'em if I want to? Who's to stop me?"

"I, your lordship—if I ever 'as any influence with 'uman nature!" returned Borkins, vehemently. "The story's common knowledge, Sir Nigel, sir. Them there flames is supernatural. Frozen flames the villagers calls 'em, because they don't seem to give out no 'eat. That part of the Fens in unin'abited and there isn't a soul in the whole village as would venture anywhere near it after dark."

"Why?"

"Because they never comes back, that's why, sir!" said Borkins. "'Tisn't any old wives' tale neither. There's been cases by the score. Only a matter of six months ago one of the boys from the mill, who was somewhat the worse for liquor, said he was a-goin' ter see who it was wot made them flames light up by theirselves, and—he never came back. And that same night another flame was added to the number!"

"Whew! Bit of a tall story that, Borkins!" Nevertheless a cold chill crept over Merriton's bones and he gave a forced, mirthless laugh.

"As true as the gospel, Sir Nigel!" said Borkins, solemnly. "That's what always 'appens. Every time any one ventures that way—well, they're a-soundin' their own death-knell, so to speak, and you kin see the new light appear. But there's never no trace of the person that ventured out across the Fens at evening time. He, or she—a girl tried it once, Lord save 'er!—vanishes off the face of the earth as clean as though they'd never been born. Gawd alone knows what it is that lives there, or what them flames may be, but I tells you it's sheer death to attempt to see for yourself, so long as night lasts. And in the morning—well, it's gone, and there isn't a thing to be seen for the lookin'!"

"Merciful powers! What a peculiar thing!" Despite his mockery of the supernatural, Merriton could not help but feel a sort of awe steal over him, at the tale as told by Borkins in the eeriest hour of the whole twenty-four—that which hangs between darkness and dawn. Should he go or shouldn't he? He was a fool to believe the thing, and yet—He certainly didn't want to die yet awhile, with Antoinette Brellier a mere handful of yards away from him, and all the days his own to cultivate her acquaintance in.

"You've fairly made my flesh creep with your beastly story!" he said, in a rather high-pitched voice. "Might have reserved it until morning—after my *début* in this haunt of spirits, Borkins. Consider my nerves. India's made a hash of 'em. Get back to bed, man, and don't worry over my investigations. I swear I won't venture out, to-night at any rate. Perhaps to-morrow I may have summoned up enough courage, but I've no fancy for funerals yet awhile. So you can keep your pleasant little reminiscences for another time, and I'll give you my word of honour that I'll do nothing rash!"

Borkins gave a sigh of relief. He passed his hand over his forehead, and his eyes—rather shifty, rather narrow, pale blue eyes which Merriton had instinctively disliked (he couldn't tell why)—lightened suddenly.

"Thank Gawd for that, sir!" he said, solemnly. "You've relieved my mind on that score. I've always thought—your poor uncle, Sir Joseph Merriton—and those flames there might 'ave been the reason for his disappearance, though of course—"

"What's that?" Merriton turned round and looked at him, his brow furrowed, the whole personality of the man suddenly awake. "My uncle, Borkins? How long have these—er—lights been seen hereabouts? I don't remember them as a child."

"Oh, mostly always, I believe, sir; though they ain't been much noticed before the last four years," replied Borkins. "I think—yes— come August next. Four years—was the first time my attention was called to 'em."

Merriton's laugh held a note of relief.

"Then you needn't have worried. My uncle has been missing for a little more than *five* years, and that, therefore, when he did disappear the flames obviously had nothing to do with it!"

Borkins's wrinkled, parchment-like cheeks went a dull, unhealthy red. He opened his mouth to speak and then drew back again. Merriton gave him a keen glance.

"Of course, how foolish of me. As you say, sir, impossible!" he stammered out, bowing backward toward the door. "I'll be getting back to my bed again, and leave you to finish your rest undisturbed. I'm sorry to 'ave troubled you, I'm sure, sir, only I was afraid something 'ad 'appened."

"That's all right. Good-night," returned Merriton curtly, and turned the key in the lock as the door closed. He stood for a moment thinking, his eyes upon the winking, flickering points of light that seemed dimmer in the fast growing light. "Now why did he make that bloomer about dates, I wonder? Uncle's been gone five years— and Borkins knew it. He was here at the time, and yet why did he suggest that old wives' tale as a possible solution of the disappearance? Borkins, my lad, there's more behind those watery blue eyes of yours than men may read. Hmm! ... Now I wonder why the deuce he lied to me?"

CHAPTER III

SUNSHINE AND SHADOW

When Merriton shaved himself next morning he laughed at the reflection that the mirror cast back at him. For he looked for all the world as though he had been up all night and his knee was painful and rather stiff, as though he had strained some ligament in it.

"Beastly place is beginning to make its mark on me already!" he said, as he lathered his chin. "My eyes look as though they had been stuck in with burnt cork, and—the devil take my shaky hand! And that railroad business yesterday helps it along. A nice state of affairs for a chap of my age, I must say! Scared as a kid at an old wives' story. Borkins is a fool, and I'm an idiot. … Damn! there's a bit off my chin for a start. I hope to goodness no one takes it into their heads to pay me a visit to-day."

His hopes, however, in this direction were not to be realized, for as the afternoon wore itself slowly away in a ramble round the old place, and through the stables—which in their day had been famous—the big, harsh-throated doorbell rang, and Merriton, in the very act of telling Borkins that he was officially "not in," happened to catch a glimpse of something light and fluffy through the stained-glass of the door, and suddenly kept his counsel.

A few seconds later Borkins ushered in two visitors. Merriton, prepared by the convenient glass for the appearance of one was nevertheless not unpleased to see the other. For the names that Borkins rolled off his tongue with much relish were those of "Miss Brellier and Mr. Brellier, sir."

His lady of the thrice blessed wreck! His lady of the dainty accent and glorious eyes.

His face glowed suddenly and he crossed the big room in a couple of strides and in the next second was holding Antoinette's hand rather longer than was necessary, and was looking down into the rouguish greeny-gray eyes that had captivated him only yesterday, when for one terrible, glorious moment he had held her in his arms, while the railroad coach dissolved around them.

"Are you fit to be about?" he said, his voice ringing with the very evident pleasure that he felt at this meeting with her, and his eyes wandering to where a strip of pink court plaster upon her forehead showed faintly through the screen of hair that covered it. Then he dropped her hand and turned toward the man who stood a pace or two behind her tiny figure, looking at him with the bluest, youngest eyes he had ever looked into.

"Mr. Brellier, is it not? Very good of you, sir, to come across in this neighbourly fashion. Won't you sit down?"

"Yes," said Antoinette, gaily, "my uncle. I brought him right over by telling him of our adventure."

The man was tall and heavily built, with a wealth of black hair thickly streaked with gray, and a trim, well-kept "imperial" which gave him the foreign air that his name carried out so well. His morning suit was extremely well cut, and his whole bearing that of the well-to-do man about town. Merriton registered all this in his mind's eye, and was secretly very glad of it. They were two thoroughbreds—that was easy to see.

And as for Antoinette! Well, he could barely keep his eyes from her. She was lovelier than ever, and clad this afternoon in all the fluffy femininity that every man loves. Anything more intoxicatingly delicious Merriton had never seen outside of his own dreams.

"It was certainly ripping of you both to come," he said nervously, feeling all hands and feet. "Never saw such a lonely spot in all my life, by George, as this house! It fairly gives you the creeps!"

"Indeed?" Brellier laughed in a deep, full-throated voice. "For my part the loneliness is what so much appeals to me. When one has spent a busy life travelling to and fro over the world, m'sieur, one can but appreciate the peaceful backwaters which are so often to be found in this very dear, very delightful England of yours. But that is not the mission upon which I come. I have to thank you, sir, for the great kindness and consideration you displayed to my niece yesterday."

His English was excellent, and he spoke with the clipped, careful accent of the foreigner, which Merriton found fascinating. He had already succumbed to something of the same thing in Antoinette. He was beginning to enjoy himself very much indeed.

"There was no need for thanks—none at all. … What is your opinion of the Towers, Miss Brellier?" he asked suddenly, leaning forward toward her, anxious to change the conversation.

She shrugged her shoulders.

"That is hardly a fair question to ask!" she responded, "when I have been in it but a matter of five minutes or more. But everything to me is enchanting! The architecture, the furnishings, the very atmosphere—"

"Brrh! If you could have been here last night!" He gave a mock shudder and broke it with a laugh. "Why, a truly haunted house wasn't a patch on it! If this place hasn't got a ghost, well then I'll eat my hat! I could fairly hear 'em, dozens and dozens of them, clinking and clanking all over the place. And if you could see my room! I sleep in a four-poster as big as a suburban villa, and every now and again the furniture gives a comfy little crack or two, like someone practising with a pistol, just to remind me that my great-great-great-grandmother's ghost is sitting in the wardrobe and watching over me with true great-etc.-grandmotherly conscientiousness. … I say, do you ride? There ought to be some rippin' rides round here, if my memory doesn't fail me."

She nodded, and the conversation took a turn that Sir Nigel found more than pleasant, and the time passed most agreeably.

Merriton, only anxious to entertain his guests, suddenly exploded the bomb which shattered that afternoon's enjoyment for all three of them.

"By the way," he remarked, "last night, while I was lying awake I saw a lot of funny flames dancing up and down upon the horizon. Seemed as though they lay in the marshes between your place and mine, Mr. Brellier. Borkins pulled a long story about 'em with all the usual trimmin's. Said they were supernatural and all that. Ever seen 'em yourself? I must say they gave me a bit of a turn. I'm not keen on spirits—except in bottle form (which by the way is a rotten bad pun, Miss Brellier,) but in India one gets chockful of that sort of thing, and there never seems to be any rational explanation. It leaves you feeling funny. What's your opinion of 'em? For seen 'em you must have done, as they seem to be the talk of the whole village from what Borkins says."

Antoinette's spoon tinkled in the saucer of the tea-cup she was holding and her face went white. Brellier shifted his eyes. A sort of tension had settled suddenly over the pleasant room.

"I—well, to tell you the truth, I can't explain 'em myself!" Brellier said at last, clearing his throat with signs of genuine nervousness. "They seem to be inexplicable. I have seen them—yes, many, many times. And so has 'Toinette, but the stories afloat about them are rather—unpleasant, and like a wise man I have kept myself free of investigation. I do hope you'll do the same, Sir Nigel. One never knows, and although one cannot always believe the silly things which the villagers prattle about, it is as well to be on the safe side. As you say, these things sometimes lack a rational explanation. I should be sorry to think you were likely to run into any unnecessary danger." He bent his head and Merriton could see that his fingers twitched.

"Borkins actually told me stories of people who had disappeared in a mysterious manner and were never found again," he remarked casually.

Brellier shrugged his shoulders. He spread out his hands.

"Among the uneducated—what would you? But it is so, even since I myself have been in residence at Withersby Hall—something like three and a half years—there have been several mysterious disappearances, Sir Nigel, and all directly traceable to a foolhardy desire to investigate these phenomena. For myself, I leave well enough alone. I trust you are going to do likewise?"

His eyes searched Merriton's face anxiously. There was a worried furrow between his brows.

Merriton laughed, and at the sound, 'Toinette, who had sat perfectly still during the discussion of the mystery, gave a little cry of alarm and covered her ears with her hands.

"I beg of you," she broke out excitedly, "please, please do not talk about it! The whole affair frightens me! Uncle will laugh I know, but—I am terrified of those little flames, Sir Nigel, more terrified than I can say! If you speak of them any more, I must go—really! Please, *please* don't dream of trying to find out what they are, Sir Nigel! It—it would upset me very much indeed if you attempted so foolish a thing!"

Merriton's first sensation at hearing this was pleasure that he was capable of upsetting her over his own personal welfare. Then the something sinister about the whole story, which seemed to affect every one with whom he came into touch, swept over him. A number of otherwise rational human beings scared out of their wits over some mysterious flames on the edge of the Fens at night time, seemed, in the face of this glorious summer's afternoon, to be little short of ridiculous. He tried to throw the idea off but could not. 'Toinette's pale face kept coming before him; the sudden dropping of her spoon struck an unpleasant chord in his memory. Brellier's attitude merely added fuel to the fire and soon they rose to go, Merriton following them to the door.

"Don't forget, then, Miss Brellier, that you are booked to me for a ride on Thursday," he said, laughingly.

She nodded to him and gave his hand a little squeeze at parting.

"I shall not forget, Sir Nigel. But—you will promise me," her voice dropped a tone or two, "you will promise me that you will not try and find out what those—those flames are, won't you? I could not sleep if you did." And they were gone.

Merriton stood awhile in silence, his brows puckered and his mouth stern. First Borkins, and then Brellier, and now—*her*! All of them begging him almost upon their knees to forego a perfectly harmless little quest of discovery. There seemed to his mind something almost fishy about it all. What then were these "Frozen Flames"? What secret did they hide? And what malignant power dwelt behind the screen of their mystery?

CHAPTER IV

AN EVIL GENIUS

Thus, despite the bad beginning at Merriton Towers the weeks that followed were filled with happiness for Merriton. His acquaintance with 'Toinette flourished and that charming young woman grew to mean more and more to the man who had led such a lonely life.

And so one day wove itself into another with the joy of sunlight over both their lives. He took to going regularly to Withersby Hall, and became an expected guest, dropping in at all hours to wile away an hour or two in 'Toinette's company, or else to have a quiet game of billiards with Brellier, or a cigar in company with both of them, in the garden, while the sun was still up. He never mentioned the flames to them again. But he never investigated them either. He had promised 'Toinette that, though he often watched them from his bedroom window, at night, watched them and wondered, and thought a good deal about Borkins and how he had lied to him about his uncle's disappearance upon that first night. Between Borkins and himself there grew up a spirit of distrust which he regretted yet did nothing to counteract. In fact it is to be feared that he did his best at times to irritate the staid old man who had been in the family so long. Borkins *did* amuse him, and he couldn't help leading him on. Borkins, noting this attitude, drew himself into himself and his face became mask-like in its impassivity.

But if Borkins became a stone image whenever Merriton was about, his effusiveness was over-powering at such times as Mr. Brellier paid a visit to the Towers. He followed both Brellier and his niece wherever they went like a shadow. Jokingly one day, Merriton had made the remark: "Borkins might be your factotum rather than mine, Mr. Brellier; indeed I've no doubt he would be, if the traditions of the house had not so long lain in his hands." He was rewarded for this remark by a sudden tightening of Brellier's lips, and then by an equally sudden smile. They were very good friends these days— Brellier and Merriton, and got on very excellently together.

And then, as the days wore themselves away and turned into months, Merriton woke up to the fact that he could wait no longer before putting his luck to the test so far as 'Toinette was concerned.

He had already confided his secret to Brellier, who laughed and patted him on the back and told him that he had known of it a long time and wished him luck. It wasn't long after this he was telling Brellier the good news that 'Toinette had accepted, and the two of them came to tell him of their happiness.

"So?" Mr. Brellier said quietly. "Well, I am very, very glad. You have taken your time, *mes enfants*, in settling this greatest of all questions, but perhaps you have been wise. … I am very happy for you, my 'Toinette, for I feel that your future is in the keeping of a good and true man. There are all too few in the world, believe me! …

"'Toinette, a friend awaits you in the drawing-room. Someone, I fear me, who will be none too pleased to hear this news, but that's as may be. Dacre Wynne is there, 'Toinette."

At the name a chill came over Merriton.

Dacre Wynne! And here! Impossible, and yet the name was too uncommon for it to be a different person from the man who always seemed somehow to turn up wherever he, Merriton, might chance to be. Sort of a fateful affinity. Good friends and all that, but somehow the things he always wanted, Dacre Wynne had invariably come by just beforehand. There was much more than friendly rivalry in their acquaintanceship. And once, as mere youngsters of seventeen and eighteen, there had been a girl, *his* girl, until Dacre came and took her with that masterful way of his. There was something brutally over-powering about Dacre, hard as granite, forceful, magnetic. To Nigel's young, clean, wholesome mind, little given to morbid imaginings as it was, it had almost seemed as if their two spirits were in some stifling stranglehold together, wrapt about and intertwined by a hand operating by means of some unknown medium. And now to find him here in his hour of happiness. Was this close, uncomfortable companionship of the spirit to be forced on him again? If Wynne were present he felt he would be powerless to avoid it.

"Do you know Dacre Wynne?" he asked, his voice betraying an emotion that was almost fear.

'Toinette Brellier glanced at her uncle, hesitated, and then murmured: "Yes—I—do. I didn't know you did, Nigel. He never spoke of you. I—he—you see he wants me, too, Nigel, and I am almost afraid to tell him—about us. But I—I have to see him. Shall I tell him?"

"Of course. Poor chap, I am sorry for him. Yes, I know him,

'Toinette. But I cannot say we are friends. You see, I—Oh, well, it doesn't matter."

But how much Dacre Wynne was to matter to him, and to 'Toinette, and to the public, and to far away Scotland Yard, and to the man of mystery, Hamilton Cleek, not they—nor any one else—could possibly tell.

They went into the long, cool drawing room together, and came upon Dacre Wynne, clad in riding things, and looking, just as Nigel remembered he always looked, very bronzed and big and handsome in a heavy way. His back was toward them and his eyes were upon a photo of 'Toinette that stood on a carved secrétaire. He wheeled at the sound of their footsteps and came forward, his face lighting with pleasure, his hand outstretched. Then he saw Merriton behind 'Toinette's tiny figure, and for a moment some of the pleasure went out of his eyes.

"Hello," he said. "However did you get to this part of the world? You always turn up like a bad penny. … What a time you've been 'Toinette!"

Merriton greeted him pleasantly, and 'Toinette's radiant eyes smiled up into his bronzed face.

"Have I?" she said, with a little embarrassed laugh. "Well, I have been out riding—with Nigel."

"Oh, Nigel lives round here, does he?" said Wynne, with a sarcastic laugh. "Like it, old man?"

"Oh, I like it well enough," retorted Merriton. "At any rate I'll be obliged to get used to it. I've said good-bye to India for keeps, Wynne. I'm settled here for good."

Wynne swung upon his heel at the tone of Merriton's voice, and his eyes narrowed. He stood almost a head taller than Nigel—who was by no means short—and was big and broad and heavy-chested. Merriton always felt at a disadvantage.

"So? You are going to settle down to it altogether, then?" said Wynne, with an odd note in his deep, booming voice. 'Toinette sent a quick, rather scared look into her lover's face. He smiled back as though to reassure her.

"Yes," he said, a trifle defiantly. "You see, Wynne, I've come into a place near here. I'm—I'm hoping to get married soon. 'Toinette and I, you know. She's done me the honour to promise to be my wife. Congratulate me, won't you?"

It was like a blow full in the face to the other man. For a moment all the colour drained out of his bronzed cheeks and he went as white as death.

"I—I—certainly congratulate you, with all my heart," he said, speaking in a strange, husky voice. "Believe me, you're a luckier chap, Merriton, than you know. Quite the luckiest chap in the world."

He took out his handkerchief suddenly and blew his nose, and then wiped his forehead, which, Merriton noted, was damp with perspiration. Then he felt in his pockets and produced a cigarette.

"I may smoke, 'Toinette? Thanks. I've had a long ride, and a hard one. … And so you two are going to get married, are you?"

'Toinette's face, too, was rather pale. She smiled nervously, and instinctively her hand crept out and touched Merriton's sleeve. She could feel him stiffen suddenly, and saw how proudly he threw back his head.

"Yes," said 'Toinette. "We're going to be married, Dacre. And I am—oh, so happy! I know you cannot help being pleased—with that. And uncle, too. He seems delighted."

Wynne measured her with his eyes for a moment. Then he looked quickly away.

"Well, Merriton, you've got your own back for little Rosie Deverill, haven't you? Remember how heart-broken you were at sixteen, when she turned her rather wayward affections to me? Now—the tables have turned. Well, I wish you luck. Think I'll be getting along. I've a good deal of work to do this evening, and I'll be shipping for Cairo, I hope, next week. That's what I came to see you about 'Toinette, but I'm afraid I am a little—late."

"Cairo, Mr. Wynne?" Brellier had entered the room and his voice held a note of surprise. "We shall miss you—"

"Oh, you'll get on all right without me, my friend," returned Wynne with a grim smile, and a look that included all three of them in its mock amusement. "I'm not quite so much wanted as I thought. Well, Nigel, I suppose you'll be giving a dinner, the proper 'stag' party, before you become a Benedict. Sorry I can't be here to join in the revels."

He put out his hand, Nigel took it, and wrung it with a heartiness and friendship that he had never before felt; but after all he had conquered! It was he Antoinette was going to marry. His heart was brimming over with pity for the man.

"Look here," he said. "Come and dine with me at the Towers before you go, Wynne, old man. We'll have a real bachelor party as you say. All the other chaps and you, just to give you a sort of send off. What about Tuesday? I won't have you say no."

For a moment a look of friendship came into Wynne's eyes. He gazed into Merriton's, and then returned the hand-grasp frankly. It was almost as though he understood this mute apology of Nigel's, and took it at its proper value.

"Thanks, old boy. Very decent of you, I'm sure. Yes, I'd like to have a peep at the other chaps before I sail. Just for old times' sake. I've nothing special doing Tuesday that I can't put off. And so—I'll come. So long."

"Good-bye," said Merriton, rather relieved at Wynne's attitude—and yet, in spite of himself, distrusting it.

"Good-bye, 'Toinette. … It's really good-bye *this* time. And I wish you all the happiness you deserve."

"Thank you."

He looked into her eyes a moment, and then with a sudden sigh turned quickly away and went out of the room. Brellier strode after him and wrung his hand while the two that were left clung to each other in silence. It was as though an unseen, sinister presence had suddenly gone from the room. The tension was lifted, and they could breathe naturally again.

Standing together they heard the front door slam.

CHAPTER V

THE SPECTRE AT THE FEAST

Merriton, clad in his evening clothes and looking exceedingly handsome, stood by the smoking room door, with Tony West, short and thickset, wearing a suit that fitted badly and a collar which looked sizes too large for him (Merriton had long given up hope of making him visit a decent tailor) and waited for the sound of motor wheels which would announce the arrival of further guests.

It was the memorable Tuesday dinner, given in the first place for Dacre Wynne, as a sort of send off before he left for Cairo. In the second Merriton intended to break it gently to the other chaps that he was shortly to become a Benedict.

Lester Stark and Tony West, very loyal and proven friends of Nigel Merriton, had arrived the evening before. Dacre Wynne was coming down by the seven o'clock train, Dicky Fordyce, Reginald Lefroy—both fellow officers of Merriton's regiment, and home on leave from India—and mild old Dr. Bartholomew, whom everyone respected and few did not love, and who was in attendance at most of the bachelor spreads in London and out of it, as being a dry old body with a wit as fine as a rapier-thrust, and a fund of delicate, subtle humour, made up the little party.

The solemn front door bell of Merriton Towers clanged, and Borkins, very pompous and elegant, flung wide the door. Merriton saw Wynne's big, broad-shouldered figure swathed in the black evening cloak which he affected upon such occasions, and which became him mightily, and with an opera hat set at the correct angle upon his closely-clipped dark hair, step into the lighted hallway, and begin taking off his gloves.

Tony West's raspy voice chimed out a welcome, as Merriton went forward, his hand outstretched.

"Hello, old man!" said Tony. "How goes it? Lookin' a bit white about the gills, aren't you, eh?… Whew! Merriton, old chap, that's my ribs, if you don't mind. I've no penchant for your bayonet-like elbow to go prodding into 'em!"

Merriton raised an eyebrow, frowned heavily, and by every other method under the sun tried to make it plain to West that the topic was taboo. Wherefore West raised *his* eyebrows, began to make a hasty exclamation, thought better of it, and then clapping his hand over his mouth broke into whistling the latest jazz tune, as though he had completely extricated both feet from the unfortunate mire he had planted them in—but with very little success.

Wynne was a frowning Hercules as he entered the pleasant smoke-filled room. Merriton's arm lay upon his sleeve, and he endured because he had to—that was all.

"Hello!" he said, to Lester Stark's rather half-hearted greeting— Lester Stark never had liked Dacre Wynne and they both knew it. "You here as well? Merriton's giving me a send-off and no mistake. Gad! you chaps will be envying me this time next week, I'll swear! Out on the briny for a decently long trip; plenty of pretty women—on which I'm bankin' of course"—he gave Merriton a sudden, searching look, "and not a care in the world. And the white lights of Cairo starin' at me across the water. Some picture, isn't it?"

"You may keep it!" said Tony West with a shudder. "When you've smelled Cairo, Wynne, old boy, you'll come skulkin' home with your tail between your legs. A 'rose by any other name would smell as sweet,' but Cairo—parts of it mind you—well, Cairo's the stinkin'st rose I ever put my nose into, that's all!"

"There are some things which offend the nostrils more than— odours!" threw back Wynne with a black look in Nigel's direction, and with a sort of slur in his voice that showed he had been drinking more than was good for him that night. "I think I can endure the smells of Cairo after—other things. Eh, Nigel?" He forced a laugh which was mirthless and unpleasant, and Merriton, with a quick glance into his friends' faces, saw that they too had seen. Wynne was in one of his "devil" humours, and all the fun and joking and merriment in the world would never get him out of it. His pity for the man suddenly died a natural death. The very evident fact that Wynne had been drinking rather heavily merely added a further distaste to it all. He wished heartily that he had never ventured upon this act of unwanted friendliness and given a dinner in his honour. Wynne was going to be the spectre at the feast, and it looked like being a poor sort of show after all.

"Come, buck up, old chap!" broke out Tony West, the irrepressible. "Try to look a little less like a soured lemon, if you can! Or we'll begin to think that you've been and gone and done something you're sorry for, and are trying to work it off on us instead."

"Hello, here's Doctor Johnson," as the venerable Bartholomew entered the room. "How goes it to-night, sir? A fine night, what? Behold the king of the feast, his serene and mighty—oh extremely mighty!—highness Prince Dacre Wynne, world explorer and soon to be lord-high-sniffer of Cairo's smells! Don't envy him the task, do you?"

He bowed with a flourish to the doctor who chuckled and his keen eyes, fringed with snow-white lashes, danced. He wore a rather long, extremely untidy beard, and his shirt-front as always was crumpled and worn. Anything more unlike a doctor it would be hard to imagine. But he was a clever one, nevertheless.

"Well, my talkative young parrot," he greeted West affectionately, "and how are you?… And who's party is this, anyhow? Yours or Merriton's? You seem to be putting yourself rather more to the fore than usual."

"Well, I'll soon be goin' aft," retorted West with a wide grin. "When old Nigel gets his innings. He's as chockful of news as an egg is of meat." West was one of the chosen few who had already heard of Nigel's engagement, and he was rather like a gossipy old woman—but his friends forgave it in him.

Merriton gave him a shove, and he fell back upon Wynne, emitting a portentous groan.

"What the devil—?" began that gentleman, in a testy voice.

Tony grinned.

"Nigel was ever thus!" he murmured, with uplifted eyes.

"Shut up!" thundered Stark, clapping a hand over West's mouth, and he subsided as the doorbell rang again, and Borkins ushered in Fordyce and Lefroy, two slim-hipped, dapper young gentlemen with the stamp of the army all over them. The party thus complete, Borkins gravely withdrew, and some fifteen minutes later the great gong in the hallway clanged out its summons. They streamed into the dining room, Doctor Bartholomew upon Tony West's fat little arm; Fordyce and Lefroy, side by side, hands in pockets and closely cropped heads nodding vigorously; Merriton and Lester Stark sauntering one slightly behind the other, and exchanging pleasantries as they went; and just in front of them, Dacre Wynne, solitary, huge, sinister, and overbearing.

Wynne sat in the seat of honour on Merriton's right. The rest sorted themselves out as they wished, and made a good deal of noise and fun about it, too. Down the length of the long, exquisitely decorated table Merriton looked at his guests and thought it wasn't going to be so dismal after all.

Champagne ran like water and spirits ran high. They joyfully toasted Wynne, and later on the news that Merriton imparted to them. In vain Dacre Wynne's low spirits were apparent. He must get over his grouch, that was all. Then once again the spirit of evil descended upon the gathering and it was Stark who precipitated its flight. "By the way, Nigel," he asked suddenly, "isn't there some ghost story or other pertaining to your district? Give us a recital of it, old boy. Walnuts and wine and ghost stories, you know, are just the right sort of thing after a dinner like this. Tony, switch off the lights. This old house of yours is the very place for ghosts. Now let us have it."

"Hold on," Nigel remonstrated. "Give me a chance to digest my dinner, and—dash it all, the thing's so deuced uncanny that it doesn't bear too much laughing at either!"

"Come along!" Six voices echoed the cry. "We're waiting, Nigel."

So Merriton had forthwith to oblige them. He, too, had had enough to drink—though drinking too heavily was not one of his vices—and his flushed face showed the excitement that burned within him.

"Come over here by the window and see the thing for yourselves, and then you shall hear the story," he began enigmatically.

Nigel pushed back the heavy curtain and there, in the darkness without—it was getting on toward ten o'clock—gleamed and danced and flickered the little flames that had so often puzzled him, and filled his soul with a strange sort of supernatural fear. Against the blackness beyond they hung like a chain of diamonds irregularly strung, flickering incessantly.

Every man there, save one, and that one stood apart from the others like some giant bull who deigns not to run with the herd—gave an involuntary exclamation.

"What a deuced pretty sight!" remarked Fordyce, in his pleasant drawl. "What is it? Some sort of fair or other? Didn't know you had such things in these parts."

"We don't." It was Merriton who spoke, rather curtly, for the remark sounded inane to his ears.

"It is no fair you ass, it's—God knows what! That's the point of the whole affair. What *are* those flames, and where do they come from? That part of the Fens is uninhabited, a boggy, marshy, ghostly spot which no one in the whole countryside will cross at night. The story goes that those who do—well they never come back."

"Oh, go easy, Nigel!" struck in Tony West with a whistle of pretended astonishment. "Champagne no doubt, but—"

"It's the truth according to the villagers, anyhow!" returned Merriton, soberly. "That is how the story goes, my lad, and you chaps asked me for it. Those Frozen Flames—it's the villagers' name, not mine—they say are supernatural phenomena, and any one, as I said before, crossing the place near them at night disappears clean off the face of the earth. Then a new flame appears, the soul of the johnny who has 'gone out'."

"Any proof?" inquired Doctor Bartholomew suddenly, stroking his beard, and arching his bushy eyebrows, as if trying to sympathize with his host's obvious half belief in the story.

Nigel wheeled and faced him in the dim light. The pupils of his eyes were a trifle dilated.

"Yes, so I understand. Short time back a chap went out—fellow called Myers—Will Myers. He was a bit drunk, I think, and thought he'd have a shot at makin' the village busybodies sit up and give 'em something to talk about. Anyhow, he went."

"And he came back?" Unconsciously a little note of anxiety had crept into Tony West's voice.

"No, on the contrary, he did *not* come back. They searched for his body all over the marshes next day, but it had disappeared absolutely, and the chap who told me said he saw another light come out the next night, and join the rest of 'em. … There, there's your story, Lester, make what you like of it. I've done my bit and told it anyway."

For a moment there was silence. Then Stark shook himself.

"Gad, what an uncanny story! Turn up the lights someone, and dispel this gloom that seems to have settled on everyone! What do you make of it?"

Suddenly Wynne's great, bulky figure swung free from the shadows. There were red glints in his eyes and a sneer curled his heavy lips. He sucked his cigar and threw his head back.

"What I make of it is a whole lot of old women's damn silly nonsense!" he announced in a loud voice. "And how a sensible, decent thinkin' man can give credence to the thing for one second beats me completely! Nigel's head was always full of imaginations (of a sort) but how you other chaps can listen to the thing—Well, all I can say is you're the rottenest lot of idiots I've ever come across!"

Merriton shut his lips tightly for a moment, and tried hard to remember that this man was a guest in his house. It was so obvious that Wynne was trying for a row, Doctor Bartholomew turned round and lifted a protesting hand.

"Don't you think your language is a trifle—er—overstrong, Wynne?" he said, in that quiet voice of his which made all men listen and wonder why they did it

Wynne tossed his shoulders. His thick neck was rather red.

"No, I'm damned if I do! You're men here—or supposed to be—not a pack of weak-kneed women!... Afraid to go out and see what those lights are, are you? Well, I'm not. Look here. I'll have a bet with you boys. Fifty pounds that I get back safely, and dispel the morbid fancies from your kindergarten brains by tellin' you that the things are glow-worms, or some fool out for a practical joke on the neighbourhood—which has fallen for it like this sort of one-horse hole-in-the-corner place would! Fifty pounds? What say you?"

He glowered round upon each of them in turn, his sneering lips showing the pointed dogs' teeth behind them, his whole arrogant personality brutally awake. "Who'll take it on? You Merriton? Fifty pounds, man, that I don't get back safely and report to you chaps at twelve o'clock to-night."

Merriton's flushed face went a shade or two redder, and he took an involuntary step forward. It was only the doctor's fingers upon his coat-sleeve that restrained him. Then, too, he felt some anxiety that this drunken fool should attempt to do the very thing which another drunken fool had attempted three months back. He couldn't bet on another man's chance of life, like he would on a race-horse!

"You'll be a fool if you go, Wynne," he said, as quietly as his excitement would permit. "As my guest I ask you not to. The thing may be all rubbish—possibly is—but I'd rather you took no chances. Who it is that hides out there and kills his victims or smuggles them away I don't know, but I'd rather you didn't, old chap. And I'm not betting on a fellow's life. Have another drink man, and forget all about it."

Wynne took this creditable effort at reconciliation with a harsh guffaw. He crossed to Nigel and put his big, heavy hands upon the slim shoulders, bending his flushed face down so that the eyes of both were almost upon a level.

"You little, white-livered sneak," he said in a deep rumbling voice that was like thunder in the still room. "Pull yourself together and try to be a man. Take on the bet or not, whichever you like. You're savin' up for the housekeepin' I suppose. Well, take it or leave it— fifty pounds that I get back safe in this house to-night. Are you on?"

Merriton's teeth bit into his lips until the blood came in the effort at repression. He shook Wynne's hands off his shoulders and laughed straight into the other man's sneering face.

"Well then go—and be damned to you!" he said fiercely. "And blame your drunken wits if you come to grief. I've done my best to dissuade you. If you were less drunk I'd square the thing up and fight you. But I'm on, all right. Fifty pounds that you don't get back here—though I'm decent enough to hope I'll have to pay it. That satisfy you?"

"All right." Wynne straightened himself, took an unsteady step forward toward the door, and it was then that they all realized how exceedingly drunk the man was. He had come to the dinner in a state of partial intoxication, which merely made him bad-tempered, but now the spirits that he had partaken of so plentifully was burning itself into his very brain.

Doctor Bartholomew took a step toward him.

"Dash it all!" he said under his breath and addressing no one in particular, "he can't go like that. Can't some of us stop him?"

"Try," put in Lester Stark sententiously, having had previous experiences of Wynne's mood, so Doctor Bartholomew did try, and got cursed for his pains. Wynne was struggling into his great, picturesque cloak, a sinister figure of unsteady gait and blood-shot eye. As he went to the hall and swung open the front door, Merriton made one last effort to stop him.

"Don't be a fool, Wynne," he said anxiously. "The game's not worth the candle. Stay where you are and I'll put you up for the night, but in Heaven's name don't venture out across the Fens now."

Wynne turned and showed him a reddened, congested face from which the eyes gleamed evilly. Merriton never forgot that picture of him, or the sudden tightening of the heart-strings that he experienced, the sudden sensation of foreboding that swept over him.

"Oh—go to hell!" Wynne said thickly. And plunged out into the darkness.

CHAPTER VI

A SHOT IN THE DARK

The church clock, some distance over Herne's Hill which lies at the back of Merriton Towers, broke the half silence that had fallen upon the little group of men in the warm smoking room with twelve sonorous, deep-throated notes. At sound of them Merriton got to his feet and stretched his hands above his head. A damper had fallen over the spirits of his guests after Wynne had gone out into the night on his foolish errand, and the fury against him that had stirred Nigel's soul was gradually wearing off.

"Well, Wynne said twelve, didn't he?" he remarked, with a sort of half-laugh as he surveyed the grave faces of the men who were seated in a semi-circle about him, "and twelve it is. We'll wait another half hour, and then if he doesn't come we'll make a move for bed. He'll be playing some beastly trick upon us, you may be sure of that. What a horrible temperament the man has! He was supposed to be putting up with the Brelliers to-night—old man Brellier was decent enough to ask him—and possibly he'll simply turn in there and laugh to himself at the picture of us chaps sitting here in the mornin' and waitin' for his return!"

Doctor Bartholomew shook his white head with a good deal of obstinacy.

"I think you're wrong there Nigel. Wynne is a man of his word, drunk or sober. He'll come back, no doubt. Unless something has happened to him."

"And this from our sceptical disbeliever, boys!" struck in Tony West, raising his hands in mock horror. "Nigel, m'lad, you've made an early conversion. The good doctor has a sneaking belief in the story. How now, son? What's your plan of action?"

"Half an hour's wait more, and then to bed," said Merriton, tossing back his head and setting his jaw. "I offered Wynne a bed in the first place, but he saw fit to refuse me. If he hasn't made use of this opportunity to turn in at the Brelliers' place, I'll eat my hat. What about a round of cards, boys, till the time is up?"

So the cards were produced, and the game began. But it was a half-hearted attempt at best, for everyone's ear was strained for the front-door bell, and everyone had an eye half-cocked toward the window. Before the half hour was up the game had fizzled out. And still Dacre Wynne did not put in an appearance.

Borkins, having been summoned, brought in some whisky and Merriton remarked casually:

"Mr. Wynne has ventured out to try and discover the meaning of the Frozen Flames, Borkins. He'll be back some time this evening— or rather morning, I should say, for it's after midnight—and the other gentlemen and myself are going to make a move for bed. Keep your ears peeled in case you hear him. I sleep like the very old devil himself, when once I do get off."

Borkins, on hearing this, turned suddenly gray, and the perspiration broke out on his forehead.

"Gone, sir? Mr. Wynne—gone—out *there*?" he said in a stifled voice. "Oh my Gawd, sir. It's—it's suicide, that's what it is! And Mr. Wynne's—gone!… 'E'll never come back, I swear."

Merriton laughed easily.

"Well, keep your swearing to yourself, Borkins," he returned, "and see that the gentlemen's rooms are ready for 'em. Doctor Bartholomew has the one next to mine, and Mr. West's is on the other side. I gave Mrs. Dredge full instructions this morning. … Good-night, Borkins, and pleasant dreams."

Borkins left. But his face was a dull drab shade and he was trembling like a man who has received a terrible shock.

"There's a case of genuine scare for you," remarked Doctor Bartholomew quietly, drawing on his pipe. "That man's nerves are like unstrung wires. Hardly ever seen a chap so frightened in all the course of my medical career. He's either had experience of the thing, or he knows something about it. Whichever way it is, he's the most terrified object I've ever laid eyes on!"

Merriton broke into a laugh. But there was not much merriment in it, rather a note of uneasiness which made Tony West glance up at him sharply.

"Best place for *you*, old chap, is your bed," he said, getting to his feet and laying an arm across Nigel's shoulders. "Livin' down here does seem to play the old Harry with one's nerves. I'm as jumpy as a kitten myself. Take it from me, Wynne will return, Nigel, and when he does he'll see to it that we all hear him. He'll probably break every pane of glass in the place with a stone, and play a devil's dance upon the knocker. That's his usual way of expressin' his pleasure, I believe. Here, here's health to you, old boy, and happiness, and the best of luck."

That little ceremony being over, they turned in, Doctor Bartholomew, his arm linked in Nigel's going with him to his bedroom, and, in the half-dusk of the spluttering candles, they stood together at the uncurtained window and looked out in silence upon the flames, the Frozen Flames that Wynne had gone out to investigate. For quite ten minutes they stood still. Then the doctor stirred himself and broke into a little laugh.

"Well, well," he said comfortably, "whatever our friend Wynne is going to do, I don't really think we need put any credence in the story that he won't return, Nigel. So you can go to bed in comfort on that, can't you?"

Merriton nodded. Then he yawned and shut his eyes.

"What's that? Credence in the story? Of course not, Doctor. I'm not such a fool as I may look. Wynne's playing a game on us, and at this moment he is probably seated in Brellier's study having a laugh at the rest of us, waitin' up for him anxiously, like a lot of scared old women. Heigho! I'm tired. … You're interested in firearms, Doctor. Here's my little pet, my sleepin' companion, you understand, that has been with me through many a hot campaign." He leaned over and took a little revolver out of the drawer of the little cabinet that stood by the bedside. The doctor, who had a remarkably fine collection of firearms, handled it with practised hands, remarked upon its good points, cocked the tiny thing, and then lifting his head looked Nigel straight in the eyes.

"I see you keep it loaded, my boy," he said quietly.

Merriton laughed.

"Yes. Habit, I suppose. One needed a loaded revolver in the jungle where every black man's hand was against you. Nice little toy, isn't it?"

"Yes. Looks very business-like, too."

"It is. Twice now it has saved my life. I owe it a good turn. … Well," laying the thing down upon the top of the cabinet and turning to the doctor with a smile. "I suppose you'll be turning in now. Pleasant dreams, old chap, and plenty of 'em. If you hear anything of Wynne—"

"I'll let you know," broke in the doctor, returning the smile affectionately. "Good-night."

He turned and went out through the door to his own room, the next one along the hall.

Nigel, after hesitating a moment, strode over to the window. It was still as black as a pocket outside, for dawn was not due for some hours yet, and against the darkness the flames still danced their nightly revel. He shook his fist at them and then broke into a harsh laugh as the thought of Dacre Wynne came to him again. Dash the fellow! He was always, in some way or another, intruding upon his privacy, whether it was mental or otherwise. Then, as he looked, it seemed as though a fresh flame suddenly flashed out in the velvet darkness to the left of the others. To his excited fancy it looked bigger, brighter, *newer*! But that was impossible! The Fens were uninhabited.

He watched the light for a moment or two, and then suddenly, obsessed with a strange fear, strode across the room and picked up the tiny revolver.

"Damn it! I'm going silly!" he exclaimed angrily, and throwing the window open took aim, his brain on fire with the champagne and the excitement of the evening. "Now let's see if you'll go, you infernal little devil!"

His finger touched the trigger, the thing spoke softly—that was one of its chief attractions for Nigel—and spat forth a little jet of flame. And as it did so, his brain cleared like magic. He laughed and shook himself as though out of a trance into which he had fallen. The light was still there. What a fool he was, potting at glow-worms like a madman! He shut the window with a bang and started to undress, and then went over to the door as he heard the doctor's voice outside.

"Thought I heard a shot, Nigel, what—?"

"You did. I'm a silly ass and have been potting at those beastly flames," returned Merriton, shamefacedly. "For Heaven's sake, don't tell the other fellows. They'll think I've gone loony. And for a moment I believe I had. But there's no harm done."

"Potting at those flames!" The doctor's voice was almost concerned. Then he shrugged his shoulders. "Oh, well, there's nothing in it! I must say I've taken a chance shot now and again at a bird myself from my bedroom before now. Still, get to bed, Nigel, like a good fellow, and have some sleep. Here, give me the pistol. You'll be potting at me before I know where I am. I'll take it into my room, thank you!"

"Right you are!" Merriton's laugh rang more normally and the doctor nodded with pleasure. "Good-night, Doctor."

"Good-night."

Then the door closed again, and the house dropped once more into stillness. In ten minutes Merriton tumbled into bed. He slept like a log. … He hadn't seen the doctor drop that sleeping draught into that last whisky while Tony West kept him talking. That was why he slept.

Later on, however, his shame at his own foolishness in firing his pistol at mere flames of the night was the cause of grave difficulty. For when he related the story of the whole affair to Cleek's master mind he *left that out*! And very nearly was it his own undoing, for strange was to be the outcome of that shot in the night.

CHAPTER VII

THE WATCHER IN THE SHADOW

But if Merriton slept, the others of the little party did not. After his door had closed upon him they appeared from their rooms, and met by arrangement once more in the study. Doctor Bartholomew—a little late at having waited and listened for the outward result of his drug in Nigel's comforting snore—joined the group with an anxious face. There was no laughter now in the pleasant, heated smoking room. Every face there wore a look that bordered closely upon fear.

"Well, Doctor," said Tony West, as he entered the room, "what's the plan? I don't like Wynne's absence, I swear I don't. It—it looks fishy, somehow. And he was in no mood to play boyish pranks on us by turnin' in at the Brelliers' place. There's somethin' else afoot. What's your idea, now?"

The doctor considered a moment.

"Better be getting out and form a search party," he said quietly. "If nothing turns up—well, Nigel needn't know we've been out. But—there's more in this than meets the eye, boys. Frankly, I don't like it. Wynne's a brute, but he never liked practical joking. It's my private opinion that he would have returned by now—if something hadn't happened to him. We'll wait till dawn, and then we'll go. Nigel is good for some hours yet. Wynne always had a bad effect on him. Ever noticed it, West? Or you, Stark?"

The two men nodded.

"Yes," said Tony, "I have. Many times. Nigel's never the same fellow when that man's about. He's—he's got some sort of devilish influence over him, I believe. And how he hates Nigel! See his eyes to-night? He could have killed him, I believe—specially as Nigel's taken his girl."

"Yes." The doctor's voice was rather grave. "Wynne's a queer chap and a revengeful one. And he was as drunk as a beast to-night. … Well, boys we'll sit down and wait awhile."

Pipes were got out and cigarettes lighted. For an hour in the hot smoking-room the men sat, talking in undertones and smoking, or dropping off into long silences. Finally the doctor drew out his watch. He sighed as he looked at it.

"Three o'clock, and no sign of Wynne yet. We'll be getting our things on, boys."

Instantly every man rose to his feet. The tension slackened with movement. In comparative silence they stole out into the hall, threw on their coats and hats, and then Tony West nervously slid the bolts of the big front door. It creaked once or twice, but no sound from the still house answered it. West swung it open, and on the whitened step they quietly put on their shoes.

The doctor switched on an electric torch and threw a blob of light upon the gravelled pathway for them to see the descent. Then one by one they went quietly down the steps, and West shut the door behind them.

"Excellent! Excellent!" exclaimed Doctor Bartholomew, as the gate was reached with no untoward happenings. "Not a soul knows we're gone, boys. That's pretty certain. Now, then, out of the gate and turn to the right up that lane. It'll take us to the very edge of the Fens, I believe, and then our search will commence."

He spoke with assurance, and they followed him instinctively. Unconsciously they had made him captain of the expedition. But— no one had heard them, he had said? If he had looked back once when the big gate shut, he might have changed his mind upon that score. With white face pressed close against the glass of the smoking-room window, which looked directly out upon the front path, stood Borkins, watching them as though he were watching a line of ghosts on their nightly prowl.

"Good Gawd!" he ejaculated, as he discerned their dark figures and the light of the doctor's torch. "Every one of 'em gone—*every one!*" And then, trembling, he went back to bed.

But the doctor did not look back, and so the little party proceeded upon its way in comparative silence until the edge of the Fens was reached. Here, with one accord, they stopped for further instructions. Three torches made the spot upon which they stood like daylight. The doctor bent his eyes downward.

"Now, boys," he said briskly. "Keep your eyes sharp for footprints. Wynne must have struck off here into the Fens, it's the most direct course. He wouldn't have been such a duffer as to walk too far out of his way—if he was bent upon going there at all. … Hello! Here's the squelchy mark of a man's boot, and here's another!"

They followed the track onward, with perfect ease, for the marshy ground was sodden and took every footprint deeply. That some man had crossed this way, and recently, too, was perfectly plain. The footprints wavered a little that was all, showing that the man who made them was uncertain upon his feet. And Wynne had left the house by no means sober!

"It looks as though he had come here after all!" broke out Tony West, excitedly. "Why the track's as plain as the nose on your face."

They zig-zagged their tedious way out across the marshy grassland, their thin shoes squelching in the bogs, their trousers unmercifully spattered with the thick, treacley mud. They spoke little, their eyes bent upon the ground, their foreheads wrinkled. On and on and on they went, while the sky above them lightened and grew murky with the soft cloudiness of breaking dawn. The flames in the distance began to pale, and the vast stretch of Fen district before them was shrouded in a light fog, misty, unutterably ghostlike and with the chill lonesomeness of death.

"Whew! Eeriest task I've ever come across!" ejaculated Stark with a grimace as he looked up for a moment into the dull mist ahead. "If we're not all down with pneumonia to-morrow, it won't be our own faults!... Some distance, isn't it, Doctor?"

"It is," returned the doctor grimly. "What a fool the man was to attempt it!... Here's a footprint, and another."

Yes, and many another after that. They staggered on, wet, cold, uncomfortable, anxious. The doctor was a little ahead of the rest of them, Tony West came second, the others straggled a pace or two behind. Suddenly the doctor stopped and gave a hasty exclamation:

"Good Heavens above!"

They ran up to him clustering around him in their eagerness, and their torches lent their rays to make the thing he gazed at more distinguishable, while another mile away at least, the flames twinkled dimly, and slowly went out one by one as though the finger of dawn had snuffed them like candle-ends.

"What the devil is it?" demanded Tony West, getting to his knees and peering at the spot with narrowed eyes.

"Charred grass. And the end of the footprints!" It was the doctor who spoke—in a queer voice sharp with excitement. "There has been a fire here or something. And—Wynne went no farther, apparently. The ground about it is as marshy as ever, and my own footprint is perfectly clear. ... What the dickens do you make of it, eh?"

But there was no answer forthcoming. Every man stood still staring down at this strange thing with wide eyes. For what the doctor said was absolute truth. The footsteps certainly *did* end here, and in a patch of charred grass as big round as a small table. What did it mean? What could it mean, but one thing? Somehow, somewhere, Wynne had vanished. It was incredible, unbelievable, and yet—there was the evidence of their own eyes. From that spot onward the ground was wholly free of the footprints of any man, woman, or child. No mark disturbed the sodden mud of it. And yet—right here, where the grasses seemed to grow tallest, this patch was burnt off and withered as though with sudden heat.

Tony West straightened himself.

"If I didn't think the whole business was a pack of lies spun into a bigger one by a lot of village gossips, I'd—I'd begin to imagine there was something in the story after all!" he said, getting to his feet and looking at the white faces about him. "It's—it's devilish uncanny, Doctor!"

"It is that." The doctor drew a long breath and stroked his beard agitatedly. "It's so devilish uncanny that one hardly knows what to believe. If this thing had happened in the East one might have looked at it with a more fatalistic eye. But *here*—in England, no man in his senses could believe such a fool's tale as that which Nigel told us to-night. And yet—Wynne has gone, vanished! Never a trace of him, though we'll search still farther for a while, to make sure!"

They separated at once, radiating out from that sinister spot and searched and searched and searched. Not a footprint was to be found beyond the spot, not a trace of any living thing. There was nothing for it but to go back to Merriton Towers and tell their tale to Nigel.

"Old Wynne has gone, and no mistake," said Tony West, as the men began slowly to retrace their steps across the marshlands, their faces in the pale light of the early morning looking white and drawn with the excitement and strain of the night. "What to make of it all, I don't know. Apparently old Wynne went out to see the Frozen Flames and—the Frozen Flames have swallowed him up, or burnt him up, one or the other."

"And yet I can't hold any credence in the thing, no matter how hard I try!" said the doctor, shaking his head gravely, as they trudged on through the mud and mire. "And if Wynne isn't found—well, there'll be the deuce to pay with the authorities. We'll have to report to the police first thing in the morning."

"Yes, the village constable will take the matter up, and knowing the story, will put entire faith in it, and that's all the help we'll get from *him*!" supplemented West with a harsh laugh. "I know the sort. … Here's the Towers at last, and if I don't make a mistake, there's the face of old Borkins pressed against the window!"

He ran ahead of the others and took the great stone steps two at a time. But Borkins had opened the door before he reached it. His eyes stared, his mouth sagged open

"Mr. Wynne, sir? You found 'im?" he asked hoarsely.

"No. No trace whatever, Borkins. Where's your master?"

"Sir Nigel, sir? 'E's asleep, and snorin' like a grampus. This'll be a shock to 'im sir, for sure. Mr. Wynne—*gone*? 'T ain't possible!"

But Tony had pushed by him and thrown open the smoking-room door. The warm, heated atmosphere came to them comfortingly. He crossed to the table, picked up a decanter and slopped out a peg of whisky. This he drank off neat. After that he felt better. The other men straggled in after him. He faced them with set lips.

"Now," said he, "to tell Nigel."

CHAPTER VIII
THE VICTIM

Dacre Wynne had vanished, leaving behind him no trace of mortal remains, and only a patch of charred grass in the middle of the uninhabited Fens to mark the spot. And Nigel Merriton, whose guest the man was, must of necessity be told the fruitlessness of the searchers' self-appointed task. The doctor volunteered to do it.

Tony West accompanied him as far as Nigel's, and then he suddenly recollected that Merriton had locked it the night before. There was nothing for it but to hammer upon the panels, or—pick the lock.

"And he'll be sleeping like a dead man, if I know anything of sleeping draughts," said the doctor, shaking his head. "Got a penknife, West?"

West nodded. He whipped the knife out of his pocket and began methodically to work at the worn lock with all the precision of an experienced burglar. But the action brought no smile to his lips, no little mocking jest to help on the job. There was something grim in the set of West's lips, and in the tension of the doctor's slight figure. Tragedy had stalked unnoticed into the Towers that evening and they had become enmeshed in the folds of its cloak. They felt it in the cold clamminess of the atmosphere, in the quiet peace of the long corridors.

Finally the thing was done. West turned the handle and the door swung inward. The doctor crossed to the bedside and took hold of the sleeping man's shoulder. He shook it vigorously.

"Nigel!" he called sharply once or twice. "Wake up! Wake up!"

But Merriton never moved. The performance was repeated and the call was louder.

"Nigel! I say, wake up—wake up! We've news for you!"

The sleeping man stirred suddenly and wrenched his shoulder away.

"Let go of me, Wynne, damn you!" he broke out petulantly, his eyes opening. "I've beaten you this time, anyhow, so part of our score is marked off! Let go, I say—I—I—*Doctor Bartholomew*! What in Heaven's name's the matter? I've been asleep, haven't I? What is it? You look as though you had seen a ghost!"

He was thoroughly awake now, and struggled to a sitting position. The doctor's face twisted wryly.

"I—wish I had, Nigel," he said bitterly. "Even ghosts would be better than—nothing at all. We've been out searching for Wynne, and I—"

"*Been out?*"

"Yes, across the Fens. We were anxious. Wynne didn't come back, you know, and so after we'd got you to bed we thought we'd make up a search party among ourselves and look into the thing. But we haven't found him, Nigel. He's vanished—completely!"

"Impossible!"

Merriton was out of bed now, still staring sleepily at them. Something in the boyishness of him struck a chord of sympathy in the doctor's heart. He alone of all of them had guessed at the genuineness of Nigel's fear for Wynne, he alone had seen into the man's heart, and discovered the half-belief that lurked there.

"I'm afraid it's perfectly true," he said quietly, as Merriton came to him and caught him by the arm, his face white. "We followed his tracks across the Fens—it had been raining and it was extremely easy to do—until they suddenly ended in a patch of half-charred grass. It was uncanny! We made a further search to make sure, but nothing rewarded our efforts. Dacre Wynne's gone somewhere, and those devilish flames of yours will be counting another victim to their lengthening list to-night."

"Good God!"

Merriton's lips trembled, and his fingers dropped from the doctor's arm.

"But I tell you it's impossible, man!" he broke out suddenly. "The thing's beyond human credulity, Doctor."

"Well, be that as it may, the fact remains—Wynne's gone," returned the doctor gloomily. "Of course we must communicate with the police. That's the next thing to do. We'll send over to make sure Wynne isn't at the Brellier's but I think there isn't a chance of it myself. Where he did go beats me completely!"

"And it fair beats me, too!" said Merriton, in a shocked voice, beginning mechanically to struggle into his clothes. "One of you might 'phone the police—though what they'll be able to do for us I don't know. It's a one-horse show in the village, and the chap who's chief constable was the fellow who told me of the other man that disappeared, and seemed quite willing to accept a supernatural explanation. Still, of course, it's the thing to be done. … And I actually saw, with my own eyes, that new flame flash out!"

He said the last words in a sort of undertone, but the doctor heard them, and twitched up an enquiring eyebrow.

"You saw the new flame? Oh   of course. And you—never mind. Our next move is to telephone the police."

But what the police could do for them was so pitifully small as to be absurd. Constable Haggers was a man whose superstitious fear of the flames got the better of his constabulary training in every way. He said he would do what he could, but he would certainly attempt nothing until broad daylight. He believed the story in every particular and said that it was well-nigh impossible to trace the vanished man. "There had been others," was all he would say, "and never a trace of 'em 'ave we ever seen!"

Telephoning the Brelliers was a mere matter of minutes, and by that means Merriton made perfectly sure that Wynne had not put in an appearance at Withersby Hall. Brellier himself answered the phone, and said that he was just thinking that as Wynne hadn't turned up yet, they must indeed have been making a night of it at the Towers.

"However," he continued, "if you say you all retired around about one o'clock, and Wynne left you soon after ten—well, I can't think what has become of him. …"

"He went out to investigate those devilish flames!" remarked Merriton, as a rather shamefaced explanation. Then he fairly heard the wires jump with the force of Brellier's exclamation.

"Eh—what? What's that you say? He went out to investigate the flames, Merriton? What fool let him go? Surely you know the story?"

"We did. And we did our best to dissuade him, Mr. Brellier," replied Merriton wearily. "But he went. You know Dacre Wynne as well as I do. He was set upon going. But he has not come back, and some of the chaps here set up a search-party to hunt for him. They discovered nothing. Simply some charred grass in the middle of the Fens and the end of his footprints. … So he didn't come round to your place then? Thanks. I'm awfully sorry to have bothered you, but you can understand my anxiety I know. I'll keep you posted as to any news we get. Yes—horrible, isn't it? So—so beastly uncanny. …"

He hung up the receiver with a drawn face.

"Well, Wynne didn't go there, anyway," he said to the group

of men who clustered round him. "So that's done with. Now we'll just have to possess our souls in patience, and see what Constable Haggers can do for us. I vote we tumble in for forty winks before the sun gets too high in the heavens. It is the most reasonable thing to do in the circumstances."

The days that followed brought them little light upon the matter. Wynne, it proved, was a man apparently without relations, and devoid of friends. The local police could make nothing of it. They had had such cases before, and were perfectly willing to let the matter rest where it was. Interest, once so high, began to flag. The thing dropped into the commonplace, and was soon forgotten, together with the man who had caused it.

But Nigel was far from satisfied. That he and Dacre Wynne were really enemies, who had posed as friends made not a particle of difference. Dacre Wynne had disappeared during the brief time that he was a guest in Merriton's house. The subject did not die with the owner of Merriton Towers. He spent many long evenings with Doctor Bartholomew talking the thing over, trying to reconstruct it, probe into it, hunt for new clues, new anything which might lead to a solution. But such talks always came to nothing. Every stone had already been turned, and the dry dust of the highway afforded little knowledge to Merriton.

Across the clear sky of his happiness a cloud had gloomed, spoiling for a time the perfection of it. He could not think of marriage while the mystery of Dacre Wynne's death remained unsolved. It seemed unthinkable.

Tony West told him he was getting morbid about it, and to have a change.

"Come up to London and see some of your friends," was West's advice. But Merriton never took it.

'Toinette seemed the only person who understood how he felt, and the knowledge of this only served to draw them closer together. She, too, felt that marriage was for the time being unthinkable, and despite Brellier's constant urging in that direction, she held her ground firmly, telling him that they preferred to wait awhile.

"I'm going to solve the blessed thing, 'Toinette," Nigel told her over and over again during these long weeks and days that followed, "if I grow gray-headed in the attempt. Dacre Wynne was no true friend of mine, but he was my guest at the time of his disappearance, and I mean to find the reason of it."

If he had only known what the future held in store for them both, would he still have clung to his purpose? Who can tell?

It was at night that the thing obsessed him worst. When darkness had fallen Merriton would sit, evening after evening, looking out upon that same scene that he had shown his companions that eventful night. And always the flames danced on their maddening way, mocking him, holding behind the screen of their brilliancy the key to Dacre Wynne's inexplicable disappearance. Merriton would sit and watch them for hours, and sometimes find himself talking to them.

What was the matter with him? Was he going insane? Or was this Dacre Wynne's abominable idea of a revenge for having stolen 'Toinette's heart away from him? To have died and sent his spirit back to haunt the man he hated seemed to Merriton sometimes the answer to the questions which constantly puzzled him.

CHAPTER IX

THE SECOND VICTIM

The alterations at Merriton Towers were certainly a success, from the builder's point of view at any rate. White paint had helped to dispel some of its gloominess, though there were whose who said that the whole place was ruined thereby. However, it was certainly an improvement to be able to have windows that opened, and to look into rooms that beckoned you with promises of cozy inglenooks, and plenty of brilliant sunshine.

Borkins looked upon these improvements with a censorious eye. He was one of those who believed in "lettin' things be"; to whom innovation is a crime, and modernity nothing short of madness. To him the dignity of the house had gone. But when it came to Nigel installing a new staff of servants, the good Borkins literally threw up his hands and cried aloud in anguish. He did not hold with frilled aprons, any more than he held with women assuming places that were not meant for them.

But if the maids annoyed Borkins, his patience reached its breaking point when Merriton—paying a flying visit to town—returned in company with a short, thickset person, who spoke with a harsh, cockney accent, and whom Merriton introduced as his "batman", "Whatever that might be," said Borkins, holding forth to Dimmock, one of the under-grooms. James Collins soon became a necessary part of the household machinery, a little cog in fact upon which the great wheel of tragedy was soon to turn.

Within a week he was completely at home in his new surroundings. Collins, in fact, was the perfect "gentleman's servant" and thus he liked always to think himself. Many a word he and Borkins had over their master's likes and dislikes. But invariably Collins won out. While every other servant in the place liked him and trusted him, the sight of his honest, red face and his ginger eyebrows was enough to make Borkins look like a thundercloud.

The climax was reached one night in the autumn when the evening papers failed to appear at their appointed time. Collins confronted Borkins with the fact and got snubbed for his pains.

"'Ere you," he said—he hadn't much respect for Borkins and

made no attempt to hide the fact—"what the dooce 'as become of his lordship's pypers? 'Ave *you* bin 'avin' a squint at 'em, ole pieface? Jist like your bloomin' cheek!"

"Not so much of your impidence, Mr. Collins," retorted Borkins. "When you h'addresses a gentleman try to remember 'ow to speak to 'im. I've 'ad nothink whatever to do with Sir Nigel's evenin' papers, and you know it. If they're late, well, wouldn't it be worth your while to go down to the station and 'ave a gentle word or two with one of the officials there?"

"Oh well, then, old Fiddlefyce," retorted Collins, with a good-natured grin, "don't lose yer wool over it; you ain't got any ter spare. 'Is Lordship's been a-arskin' fer 'em, and like as not they ain't turned up. Let's see what's the time? 'Arf-past eight." He shook his bullet-shaped head. "Well, I'll be doin' as you say. Slap on me 'at and jacket and myke off ter the blinkin' stytion. What's the shortest w'y, Borkins, me beauty?"

Borkins looked at him a moment, and his face went a dull brick colour. Then he smirked sarcastically.

"Like as not you're so brave you wouldn't mind goin' across the Fens," he said. "Them there flames wouldn't be scarin' such a 'ero as Mr. James Collins. Oh no! You'll find it a mile or so less than the three miles by road. It's the shortest cut, but I don't recommend it. 'Owever, that lies with you. I'll tell Sir Nigel where you're gone if 'e asks me, you may be sure!"

"Orl right! Across the Fens is the shortest, you says. Well, I'll try it ternight and see. You're right fer once. I ain't afraid. It tykes more'n twiddley little bits er lights ter scare James Collins, I tells yer. So long."

Borkins, standing at the window in the dining room and peering through the dusk at Collins' sturdy figure as it swung past him down the drive, bit his lip a moment, and made as if to go after him.

"No, I'll be danged if I do!" he said suddenly. "If 'e knows such a lot, well, let 'im take the risk. I warned 'im anyhow, so I've done my bit. The flames'll do the rest." And he laughed.

But James Collins did not come back, when he ought to have done, and the evening papers arrived before him, brought by the station-master's son Jacob. Jacob had seen nothing of Collins, and Merriton, who did not know that the man had gone on this errand, made no remark when the hours went slowly by, and no sign of Collins appeared.

At eleven o'clock the household retired. Merriton, still ignorant of his man's absence, went to bed and slept soundly. The first knowledge he received of Collins' absence was when Borkins appeared in his bedroom in the morning.

"Where the deuce is Collins?" Merriton said pettishly, for he did not like Borkins, and they both knew it.

"That's exactly what I 'ave been tryin' ter find out, sir," responded Borkins, bravely. "'E 'asn't been back since last night, so far as I could make out."

"*Last night?*" Merriton sat bolt upright in bed and ran his fingers through his hair. "What the dickens do you mean?"

"Collins went out last night, sir, to fetch your papers. Leastways that was what he said he was goin' for," responded Borkins patiently, "and so far as I knows he 'asn't returned yet. Whether he dropped into a public 'ouse on the way or not, I don't know, or whether he took the short cut to the station across the Fens isn't for me to say. But—'e 'asn't come back yet, sir!"

Merriton looked anxious. Collins had a strong hold upon his master's heart. He certainly wouldn't like anything to happen to him.

"You mean to say," he said sharply, "that Collins went out last night to fetch my papers from the station and was fool enough to take the short cut across the Fens?"

"I warned him against doin' so," said Borkins, "since 'e said 'e'd probably go that way. That no Frozen Flames was a-goin' ter frighten 'im, an'—an' 'is language was most offensive. But I've no doubt 'e went."

"Then why the devil didn't you tell me last night?" exclaimed Merriton angrily, jumping out of bed. "You knew the—the truth about Mr. Wynne's disappearance, and yet you deliberately let that man go out to his death. If anything's happened to James Collins, Borkins, I'll—I'll wring your damned neck. Understand?"

Borkins went a shade or two paler, and took a step backward.

"Sir Nigel, sir—I—"

"When did Collins go?"

"'Arf past eight, sir!" Borkins' voice trembled a little. "And believe me or not, sir, I did my best to persuade Collins from doin' such an extremely dangerous thing. I begged 'im not to think o' doin' it, but Collins is pig-'eaded, if you'll forgive the word, sir, and he was bent upon gettin' your papers. I swear, sir, I ain't 'ad anythin' ter do with it, and when 'e didn't come back last night before I went to bed I said to meself, I said, 'Collins 'as dropped into a public 'ouse and made a—a ass of hisself', I said. And thought no more about it, expectin' he'd be in later. But 'is bed 'asn't been slept in, and there 's no sign of 'im anywhere."

Merriton twisted round upon his heel and looked at the man keenly for a moment.

"I'm fond of Collins, Borkins," he said abruptly. "We've known each other a long time. I shouldn't like anything to happen to the chap while he's in my service, that's all. Get out now and make enquiries in every direction. Have Dimmock go down to the village. And ransack every public house round about. If you can't find any trace of him—" his lips tightened for a moment, "then I'll fetch in the police. I'll get the finest detective in the land on this thing, I'll get Cleek himself if it costs me every penny I possess, but I'll have him traced somehow. Those devilish flames are taking too heavy a toll. I've reached the end of my tether!"

He waved Borkins out with an imperious hand, and went on with his dressing, his heart sick. What if Collins had met with the same fate as Dacre Wynne? What were those fiendish flames, anyhow, that men disappeared completely, leaving neither sight nor sound? Surely there was some brain clever enough to probe the mystery of them.

"If Collins doesn't turn up this morning," he told himself as he shaved with a very unsteady hand, "I'll go straight up to London by the twelve o'clock train and straight to Scotland Yard. But I'll find him—damn it, I'll find him."

But no trace of James Collins could be found. He was gone—completely. No one had seen him, no one but Borkins had known of his probable journey across the Fens at night-time, and Borkins excused himself upon the plea that Collins hadn't actually *said* he was going that way. He had simply vanished as Dacre Wynne had vanished, as Will Myers and all that long list of others had vanished. Eaten up by the flames—and in Twentieth Century England! But the fact remained. Dacre Wynne had disappeared, and now James Collins had followed him. And a new flame shone among the others, a newer, brighter flame than any before. Merriton saw it himself, that was the devilish part of it. His own eyes had seen the thing appear, just as he had seen it upon the night when Dacre Wynne had vanished. But he didn't shoot at it this time. Instead, he packed a small bag, ran over and said good-bye to 'Toinette and told her he was going to have a day in town, but told her nothing else. Then he took the twelve o'clock train to town. A taxi whisked him to Scotland Yard.

CHAPTER X

— AND THE LADY

And this was the extraordinary chain of events which brought young Merriton into Mr. Narkom's office that day while Cleek was sitting there, and on being introduced as "Mr. Headland" heard the story from Sir Nigel's lips.

As he came to the last "And no trace of either body has ever been found," Cleek suddenly switched round in his chair and exclaimed:

"An extraordinary rigmarole altogether!" Meeting Merriton's astonished eyes with his own keen ones, he went on: "The flames, of course, are a plant of some sort. That goes without saying. But the thing to find out is what they're there for to hide. When you've discovered that, you'll have got half way to the truth, and the rest will follow as a matter of course. … What's that, Mr. Narkom? Yes, I'll take the case, Sir Nigel. My name's Cleek—Hamilton Cleek, at your service. Now let's hear the thing all over again, please. I've one or two questions I'd like to ask."

Merriton left Scotland Yard an hour later, lighter in heart than he had been for some time—ever since, in fact, Dacre Wynne's tragic disappearance had cast such a gloom over his life's happiness. He had unburdened his soul to Cleek—absolutely. And Cleek had treated the confession with a decent sort of respect which was enough to win any chap over to him. Merriton in fact had found in Cleek a friend as well as a detective. He had been a little astonished at his general get-up and appearance, but Merriton had heard of his peculiar birthright, and felt that the man himself was capable of almost anything. Certainly he proved full of sympathetic understanding.

Cleek understood the ground upon which he stood with regard to his friendship with Dacre Wynne. He had, with a wonderful intuition, sensed the peculiar influence of the man upon Nigel—this by look and gesture rather than by use of tongue and speech. And Cleek had already drawn his own conclusions. He heard of Nigel's engagement to Antoinette Brellier, and of how Dacre Wynne had taken it, heard indeed all the little personal things which Merriton had never told to any man, and certainly hadn't intended telling to this one.

But that was Cleek's way. He secured a man's confidence and

by that method got at the truth. A bond of friendship had sprung up between them, and Cleek and Mr. Narkom had promised that before a couple of days were over, they would put in an appearance at Fetchworth, and look into things more closely. It was agreed that they were to pose as friends of Sir Nigel, since Cleek felt that in that way he could pursue his investigations unsuspected, and make more headway in the case.

But there was but one thing Nigel hadn't spoken of, and that was the very foolish and ridiculous action of his upon that fateful evening of the dinner party. Only he and Doctor Bartholomew—who was as close-mouthed as the devil himself over some things—knew of the incident of the pistol-shooting, so far as Merriton was aware. And the young man was too ashamed of the whole futile affair and what it very apparently proved to the listener—that he had certainly drunk more than was good for him—to wish any one else to share in the absurd little secret. It could have no bearing upon the affair, and if 'Toinette got to hear of it, well, he'd look all sorts of a fool, and possibly be treated to a sermon—a prospect which he did not relish in the slightest.

As he left the Yard and turned into the keen autumn sunshine, he lifted his face to the skies and thanked the stars that he had come to London after all and placed things in proper hands. There was nothing now for him to do but to go back to Merriton Towers and as expeditiously as possible make up for the day lost from 'Toinette.

So, after a visit to a big confectioners in Regent Street, and another to a little jeweller in Piccadilly, Merriton got into the train at Waterloo, carrying his parcels With a happy heart. He got out at Fetchworth station three hours later, hailed the only hack that stood there—for he had forgotten to apprise any one at the Towers of his quick return—and drove straightway to Withersby Hall.

'Toinette was at the window as he swung open the great gate. When she saw him she darted away and came flying down the drive to meet him.

The contents of the various packages made her happy as a child, and it was some time after they reached the house that Nigel asked some question concerning her uncle.

Her face clouded ever so little, and for the first time Nigel noticed that she was pale.

"Uncle has gone away for a few days," she replied. "He said it was business—what would you? But I told him I should be lonesome in this great house, and I—I am so frightened at those horrible little flames that twinkle twinkle all night long. I cannot sleep when I am alone, Nigel. I am a baby I know, but I cannot help it. It makes me feel so afraid!"

As was usual in moments of emotion with 'Toinette, her accent became more pronounced. He stroked her hair with a gentle hand, as though she were in very truth the child she tried not to be.

"Poor little one! I wish I could come across and put up here for the night. Hang conventions, anyway! And then too I have to make ready for some visitors who will be down to-morrow or the next day."

"Visitors, Nigel?"

"Yes, dear. I've a couple of—friends coming to spend a short time with me. Chaps I met in London to-day."

"What did you go up for, Nigel—really?"

He coloured a little, and was thankful that she turned away at that moment to straighten the collar of her blouse. He didn't like lying to the woman he was going to marry. But he had given his word to Cleek.

"Oh," he said off-handedly, "I—I went to my tailor's. And then stepped in to buy you that little trinket and your precious chocs, and came along home again. Met these fellows on my way across town. Rather nice chaps—one of 'em, anyhow. Used to know some friends of friends of his, girl called Ailsa Lorne. And the other one happened to be there so I asked him, too. They won't worry you much, 'Toinette. They're frightfully keen about the country, and will be sure to go out shootin' and snuffin' round like these town johnnies always do when they get in places like this. … Well, as Mr. Brellier isn't here I suppose I'd better be making my way home again. Wish we were married, 'Toinette. There'd be no more of these everlasting separations then. No more nightmares for you, little one. Only happiness and joy, and—and heaps of other rippin' things. Never mind, we'll make it soon, won't we?"

She raised her face suddenly and her eyes met his. There was a haunted look in them that made him draw closer, his own face anxious.

"What is it, dear?" he said in a low, worried tone.

"Only—Dacre Wynne. Always Dacre Wynne these days," she replied unsteadily. "Do you know, Nigel, I am a silly girl, I know, but somehow I dare not think of marriage with you until—everything is finally cleared up, and his death or disappearance, or whatever the dreadful affair was, discovered. I feel in some inexplicable way responsible. It is as if his spirit were standing between us and our happiness. Tell me I am foolish, please."

"You are more than foolish," said Nigel obediently, and laughed carelessly to show her how he treated the thing. But in his heart he knew her feelings, knew them and fully understood. It was exactly as he had felt about it also. The bond that bound Dacre Wynne's life to his had not yet been snapped, the mystery of his disappearance seemed only to strengthen it. He wondered dully when he would ever feel free again, and then laughed inwardly at himself for making a farce of the whole thing, for building a mountain out of a stupid little molehill. And 'Toinette was helping him. They were both unutterably foolish. Anyhow, Cleek was coming soon to clear matters up. He wished with all his heart that he might tell 'Toinette, and thus relieve the tension of her mind, but he had given his word to Cleek, and with a man of his type his word was sacred.

So he kissed her good-bye and laughed, and went back to Merriton Towers to prepare for their coming. But the cloud had dropped across his horizon again, and the sun was once more obscured. There was no smile upon his lips as he clanged the great front door to behind him.

CHAPTER XI
THE SECRET OF THE FLAMES

Fetchworth, as everybody knows, lies in that part of the Fen district of Lincolnshire that borders on the coast, and in the curve of its motherlike arm Saltfleet Bay, a tiny shipping centre with miniature harbour, drowses its days in pleasant idleness.

And so it was that upon the morning of Cleek's and Mr. Narkom's arrival at Merriton Towers. They came disguised as two idlers interested in the surrounding country, after having satiated themselves at the fountain of London's gaieties, and bore the pseudonyms of "George Headland" and "Mr. Gregory Lake" respectively. Cleek himself was primed, so to speak, on every point of the landscape. He knew all about Fetchworth that there was to know—saving the secret of the Frozen Flames, and that he was expected to know very soon—and the traffic of Saltfleet Bay and its tiny harbour was an open book to him.

Even Withersby Hall and its environs had had the same close intensive study, and everything that was to be learnt from guidebooks, tourists' enquiry offices and the like, was hidden away in the innermost recesses of his remarkable brain.

Borkins, standing at the smoking-room window—a favourite haunt of his from which he was able to see without too ostensibly being seen—noted their coming up the broad driveway, with something of disfavour in his look. Merriton had given him certain directions only the night before, and Borkins was a keen-sighted man. Also, the little fat johnny at any rate, didn't quite look the type of man that the Merriton's were in the habit of entertaining at the Towers.

However, he opened the door with a flourish, and told the gentlemen that "Sir Nigel is in the drorin'-room," whither he led them with much pomp.

Cleek took in the place at a glance. Noted the wide, deep hallway; the old-fashioned outlines of the house, smartened up freshly by the hands of modern workmen; the set of each door and window that he passed, and stowed away these impressions in the pigeon-holes of his mind. As he proceeded to the drawing-room he set out in his mind's eye the whole scene of that night's occurrence as had been related to him by Sir Nigel. There was the smoking-room door, open and showing the type of room behind it; there the hall-stand from which Dacre Wynne had fatefully wrenched his coat and hat, to go lurching out into oblivion, half-drunk and maddened with something more than intoxication—if Merriton had told his story truly, and Cleek believed he had. It was, in fact, in that very smoking-room that the legend which had led up to the tragedy had been told. Hmm. There certainly was much to be cleared up here while he was waiting for that other business at the War Office to adjust itself. He wouldn't find time hanging heavily upon his hands there was no doubt of that, and the thought that this man who had come to him for help was a one-time friend of Ailsa Lorne's, the one dear woman in the world, added fuel to the fire of his already awakened interest.

He greeted Merriton with all the bored ennui of the part he had adopted, during such time as he was under Borkins' watchful eye. Even Mr. Narkom played his part creditably, and won a glance of approval from his justly celebrated ally.

"Hello, old chap," said Cleek, extending a hand, and screwing a monocle still farther into his left eye. "Awfully pleased to see you, doncherknow. Devilish long journey, what? Beastly fine place you've got here, I must say. What you think, Lake?"

Merriton gasped, bit his lip, and then suddenly realizing who the gentleman thus addressing him was, made an attempt at the right sort of reply.

"Er—yes, yes, of course," he responded, though somewhat at random, for this absolutely new creature that Cleek had become rather took his breath away. "Afraid you're very tired and all that. Cold, Mr.—er Headland?"

Cleek frowned at the slight hesitation before the name. He didn't want to take chances of any one guessing his identity and Borkins was still half-way within the room, and probably had sharp ears. His sort of man had!

"Not very," he responded, as the door closed behind the butler. "At least that is, Sir Nigel,"—speaking in his natural voice—"it really was pretty chilly coming down. Winter's setting in fast, you know. That your man?"

He jerked his head in the direction of the closed door, and twitched an enquiring eyebrow.

Merriton nodded.

"Yes," he said, "that's Borkins. Looks a trustworthy specimen, doesn't he? For my part I don't trust him farther than I can see him, Mr.—er—Headland (awfully sorry but I keep forgetting your name somehow). He's too shifty-eyed for me. What do you think?"

"Tell you better when I've had a good look at him," responded Cleek, guardedly. "And lots of honest men are shifty-eyed, Sir Nigel, and vice versa. That doesn't count for anything, you know. Well, my dear Mr. Lake, finding your part a bit too much for you?" he added, with a laugh, turning to Mr. Narkom, who was sitting on the extreme edge of his chair, mournfully fingering his collar, which was higher and tighter than the somewhat careless affair which he usually adopted. "Never mind. As the poet sings, 'All the world's a stage, and all the men and women, etc.' You're simply one of 'em, now. Try to remember that. And remember, also, that the eyes of the gallery are not always upon you. Sir Nigel, I ask you, isn't our friend's make-up the perfection of the—er—elderly man-about-town?"

Sir Nigel laughingly had to admit that it was, whereupon Mr. Narkom blushed exceedingly, and—the ice was broken as Cleek had intended it should be.

They adjourned to the smoking-room, where a huge log-fire burnt in the grate, and easy chairs invited. They discussed the topics of the day with evident relish during such time as Borkins was in the room, and smoked their cigars with the air of men to whom the hours were as naught, and life simply a chessboard to move their little pieces upon as they willed. But how soon they were to cry checkmate upon this case which they were all investigating, even Cleek did not know. Then of a sudden he looked up from his task of studying the fire with knitted brows.

"By the way," he said off-handedly, "I hope you don't mind. My man will be coming down by the next train with our traps. I never travel without him, he's such a useful beggar. You can manage to put him up somewhere, I suppose? I was a fool not to have mentioned it before, but the lad entirely slipped my memory. He helps me, too, in other things, and there is always a good deal to be learned from the servants' hall, you know, Sir Nigel. … You can manage with Dollops, can't you? Otherwise he can put up at the village inn."

Merriton shook his head decisively.

"Of course not, Mr. Headland. Wouldn't hear of such a thing. Anybody who is going to be useful to you in this case is, as you know, absolutely welcome to Merriton Towers. He won't get much out of Borkins though, I don't mind telling you."

"Hmm. Well that remains to be seen, doesn't it, Mr. Narkom?" returned Cleek, with a smile. "Dollops has a way. And he knows it. I'll warrant there won't be much that Borkins can keep from the sharp little devil! Well, it seems to be getting dusk rapidly, Sir Nigel, what about those flames now, eh? I'd like to have a look at 'em if it's possible."

Merriton screwed his head round to the window, and noted the gathering gloom which the fire and the electric lights within had managed to neutralize. Then he got to his feet. There was a trace of excitement in his manner. Here was the moment he had been waiting for, and here the master-mind which, if anything ever could, must unravel this fiendish mystery that surrounded two men's disappearances and a group of silly, flickering little flames.

He turned from the window with his eyes bright.

"Look here," he said, rapidly. "They're just beginnin' to appear. See 'em? Mr. Cleek, see 'em? Now tell me what the dickens they are and how they are connected with Dacre Wynne's disappearance."

Cleek got to his feet slowly, and strode over to the window. In the gathering gloom of the early winter night, the flames were flashing out one by one, here and there and everywhere hanging low against the grass across the bar of horizon directly in front of them. Cleek stared at them for a long time. Mr. Narkom coming up behind him peered out over his shoulder, rubbed his eyes, looked again and gave out a hasty "God bless my soul!" of genuine astonishment, then dropped into silence again, his eyes upon Cleek's face. Sir Nigel, too, was watching that face, his own nervous, a trifle distraught.

But Cleek stood there at the window with his hands in his trousers' pockets, humming a little tune and watching this amazing phenomenon which a whole village had believed to be witchcraft, as though the thing surprised him not one whit; as though, in fact, he was a trifle amused at it. Which indeed he was.

Finally he swung round upon his heels and looked at each of the faces in turn, his own broadening into a grin, his eyes expressing incredulity, wonderment, and lastly mirth. At length he spoke:

"Gad!" he ejaculated with a little whistle of astonishment. "You mean to tell me that a whole township has been hanging by the heels, so to speak, upon as ridiculously easy an affair as that?" He jerked his thumb outward toward the flames and threw back his head with a laugh. "Where is your 'general knowledge' which you learnt at school, man? Didn't they teach you any? What amazes me most is that there are others—forgive me—equally as ignorant. Want to know what those flames are, eh?"

"Well, rather!"

"Well, well, just to think that you've actually been losing sleep on it! Shows what asses we human beings are, doesn't it? No offence meant, of course. As for you, Mr. Narkom—or Mr. Gregory Lake, as I must remember to call you for the good of the cause—I'm ashamed of you, I am indeed! You ought to know better, a man of your years!"

"But the flames, Cleek, the flames!" There was a tension in Merriton's voice that spoke of nerves near to the breaking point. Instantly Cleek was serious. He reached out a hand and laid it upon the young man's shoulder. Merriton was trembling, but he steadied under the grip, just as it was meant that he should.

"See here," Cleek said, bluntly, "you oughtn't to work yourself up into such a state. It's not good for you; you'll go all to pieces one of these days. Those flames, eh? Why I thought any one knew enough about natural phenomena to answer that question. But it seems I'm wrong. Those flames are nothing more nor less than marsh gas, Sir Nigel, evolved from the decomposition of vegetation, and therefore only found in swampy regions such as this. Whew! and to think that here is a community that has been bowing down to these things as symbols from another world!"

"Marsh gas, Mr.—"

"Headland, please. It is wiser, and will help better to remember when the necessity arises," returned Cleek, with a smile. "Yes, that is all they are—the outcome of marsh gas."

"But what *is* marsh gas, Mr.—Headland?" Merriton's voice was still strained.

Cleek motioned to a chair.

"Better sit down to it, my young friend," he said, gently. "Because, to one who isn't interested, it is an extremely dull subject. However, it is better that you should know—as you don't seem to have learnt it at school. Here goes: marsh gas, or methane as it is sometimes called, is the first of the group of hydrocarbons known as paraffins. Whether that conveys anything to you I don't know. But you've asked for knowledge and I mean you to have it." He smiled again, and Merriton gravely shook his head, while Mr. Narkom, dropping for the time being his air of pompous boredom, became the interested listener in every line of his ample proportions.

"Go on, old chap," he said eagerly.

"Methane," said Cleek, serenely, "is a colourless, absolutely odourless gas, slightly soluble in water. It burns with a yellowish flame—which golden tinge you have no doubt noticed in these famous flames of yours—with the production of carbonic acid and water. In the neighbourhood of oil wells in America, and also in the Caucasus, if my memory doesn't fail me, the gas escapes from the earth, and in some districts—particularly in Baku—it has actually been burning for years as sacred fires. A question of atmosphere and education, you see, Sir Nigel."

"Good Heavens! Then you mean to say that those beastly things out there are not lit by any human or superhuman agency at all!" exploded Merriton at this juncture. "And that they have nothing whatever to do with the vanishing of Wynne and Collins?"

Cleek shook his head emphatically.

"Pardon me," he said, "but I didn't say that. The first part of the sentence I agree with entirely. Those so-called flames are lit only by the hand of the Infinite. And the Infinite is always mysterious, Sir Nigel. But as to whether they have any bearing upon the disappearances of those two men is a horse of another colour. We'll look into that later on. In coal-mines marsh gas is considered highly dangerous, and the miners call it fire-damp. But that is by the way. What enters into the immediate question is the fact that there is a patch of charred grass upon the Fens where you say the vanished man, Dacre Wynne's footprints suddenly ended. Hmm."

He stopped speaking suddenly, and getting up again crossed over to the window. He stood for a moment looking out of it, his brows drawn down, his face set in the stern lines that betokened concentration of thought.

Mr. Narkom and Merriton watched him with something of wonder in their eyes. To Merriton, at any rate, who really knew so little of Cleek's unique and powerful mind, the fact of a policeman having such extensive information was surprising in the extreme.

"You don't think, then," he said, breaking the silence that had fallen upon them, "that this—er—marsh gas could have caused the death of Wynne and Collins? Burnt 'em alive, so to speak?"

Cleek did not move at this question. They merely saw his shoulders twitch as though he didn't wish to be bothered at the moment.

"Don't know," he said laconically, "and if that were true, where are the bodies?... Gad! Just as I thought! Come here, gentlemen, this may interest you. See that flame there! It's no more natural marsh gas than I am! There's human agency all right, Sir Nigel. There's natural marsh gas and there are—other things as well. Those marsh lights are being augmented. But for what purpose? What reason? That's the thing we've got to find out."

CHAPTER XII

"AS A THIEF IN THE NIGHT—"

The arrival of Dollops lighted a spark of great interest in the servants' hall. The newly engaged maids accepted him for his youth and sharp manners, as an innovation which they rather fancied than otherwise. Borkins alone stood aloof. It seemed to the man that here, in Dollops' lithe, young form, in the very ginger of his carrotty hair, in the stridency of this cockney accent—which Cleek had endeavoured to eradicate without a particle of success—was the reembodiment of the older, shorter, more mature James Collins. To hear him speak in that sharp, young voice of his was to make the hair upon one's neck prick in supernatural discomfort. It was as though James Collins had come back to life again in the form of this East Side youngster, who was so extremely unlike his drawling, over-pampered master.

But Dollops had been primed for his task, and set to work at it with a will.

"Been in these 'ere parts long, Mr. Borkins?" he queried as they all sat at supper, and he himself munched bread and butter and fish paste with a vigour that was lacking in only one quality—manners.

Borkins sniffed, and passed up his cup to the housekeeper.

"Before you were born, I dessay," he responded tartly.

"Is that so, Methuselah?" Dollops gave a little boyish giggle at sight of the butler's face. "Well, seein' as I'm gettin' along in life, you must be a good way parst the meridian, if yer don't mind my sayin' so. … Funny thing, on the way down I run across a chap wot's visitin' pals in this 'ere village, and 'e pulls me the strangest yarn as ever a body 'eard. Summink to do wiv flames it were—Frozen Flames or icicles or frost of some kind. But 'e was so full up of mystery that there weren't no gettin' nuffin out er' im. Any one 'ere tell me the story? 'E fair got me curiosity fired, 'e did!"

A glance laden with sinister meaning flew around the table. Borkins cleared his throat as every eye fastened itself upon him, and he swelled visibly beneath his brass-buttoned waistcoat.

"If you're any wiser than you look, young man, you'll leave well alone, and not go stickin' your fingers in other peoples' pie!" he gave out sententiously. "Yes, there is a story—and a very unpleasant one, too. If you use your eyes to-night and look out of the smoking-room window as dusk comes on, you'll see the Frozen Flame for yerself, and won't want to be arskin' me any fool questions about it. One of the servants 'ere—and a rude, unmannerly London creetur 'e was too!—disappeared a while ago, goin' out across the Fens after night-time when 'e was warned not to. Never seen a sight of 'im since—though I'm not mournin' any, as you kin see!"

"*Go on!*" Dollops' voice expressed incredulity, amazement, and an awed interest that rather flattered the butler.

"True as I'm sittin' 'ere!" he responded grimly. "And before that a friend of Sir Nigel's—a fine, big upstandin' man 'e were, name of Wynne—went the same way. Got a little the worse for drink and laughed at the story. Said 'e'd go out and investigate for 'imself. 'E never come back from that day to this!"

"Gawd's truf! 'Ow orful! You won't find yer 'umble a 'ankerin' after the fresh air come night-time!" broke in Dollops with a little shiver of terror that was remarkably real. "I'll keep to me downy thank you, an' as you say, Mr. Borkins, leave well enough alone. You're a wise gentleman, you are!"

Borkins, flattered, still further expanded.

"I won't say as all you cockney chaps are the same as Collins," he returned magnanimously, "for it takes all kinds ter make a world. If you feels inclined some time, I'll walk you down to the Pig and Whistle and you shall 'ave a word or two with a chap I know. 'E'll tell yer somethink that'll make your 'air stand on end. You jist trot along ter me when you're free, and we'll take a little stroll together."

Dollops' countenance widened into a delighted grin.

Later, Dollops, in the act of laying out Cleek's clothes for dinner, while Cleek himself unpacked leisurely and made the braces that held the mirror of the dressing-table gay with multi-coloured ties, gave out the news of his promised visit to the Pig and Whistle with the august Borkins with something akin to triumph.

"That's right, lad, that's right. Get friendly with 'em!" returned Cleek with a pleased smile. "I've an idea we're going to have a pretty lively time down here, if I'm not much mistaken. Stick to that chap Borkins as you would to glue. Don't let him get away from you. Follow him wherever he goes, but don't let the other servants in the place slip out from your watchful eye, either. Those Frozen Flames want looking into. I have grave suspicions of Borkins. His sort generally knows more than almost any other sort, and he appeared to be sizing me up pretty carefully. I shouldn't wonder at all, if he had an idea already that I am not the 'man about town' I appear to be. It will be rotten luck if he has. … Time I got into my togs, boy. … Here, just hand me that shirt, will you?"

That night certainly proved an even more exciting one than Cleek had prophesied. The household retired early, as country households are apt to do, but Cleek, however, did not undress. He sat at his window, which faced upon the Fens, watching the trail of the flames dancing across the horizon of night, and trying to solve the riddle that he had come to find the answer to.

He heard the church clock in the distance chime out the hour of twelve; and still he sat on. The peace of the quiet night stole over him, filling his active brain with a restfulness that had been foreign to it for some time in the stress of his busy life in London. He felt glad he had taken up this case, if only for the view of the countryside at night, the stillness of the untrod marshes, and the absolute absence of every living thing at this hour.

The clock chimed one, and he heeded it not. Two—half-past—. Of a sudden he sat bolt upright, then got noiselessly to his feet and glided across the floor to where his bed stood—a monstrous black object with heavy canopy and curtains, a relic of the Victorianism in which this house was born. He moved like a cat, absolutely without sound, fleet, sure. His fingers found the coverlet and he tore it down, tumbling the clothes and pushing down the pillow so that it looked as if he himself lay there, peacefully sleeping beneath the sheltering blankets. … Then, still noiseless, panther-like, he slid his lithe figure under the bed. … Then the noise came again. Just the whisper of footsteps in the wide hall, and then—his door opened soundlessly and for a moment the footsteps stopped. He could feel a presence in the room. If it were Dollops the lad would give some sign. If not—He lay still, scarcely breathing in the enveloping darkness. The footsteps came again, softly, softly padding across the room toward him. He saw the black shadows of stockinged feet as they crossed the path of moonlight, and sucked in his breath. Man's feet!… Whose?… Then something shook the bedstead with tremendous force, but without sound. It was as if some object had been hurled forcibly into its soft-ness. The footsteps turned again, hurriedly this time, and there was a sound of a deep-drawn breath—a breath full of pent-up, passionate hatred. Then the figure ran lightly across the room, and as it flashed for a moment through the bar of moonlight, Cleek looked out from his safe hiding-place and—*saw*! The eyes were narrowed in the ivory-tinted face, the jaw heavy and undershot as a bull-dog's, while a dark coloured mustache straggled untidily across the upper lip. The moonlight, cruelly clear, picked out the point of something sharp that shone in one clenched hand, something that looked like a knife—that *was* a knife.

Then the figure vanished and the door closed noiselessly behind him.

Hmm. So this question of the Frozen Flame was as urgent as all that, was it? To attempt to murder him, here—in the house of the Squire of Fetchworth. He wriggled out of his hiding place, a little stiff from the cramped position he had held, and guardedly lit his candle. Then he surveyed the bed with set mouth and narrowed eyes. There was a sharp incision through the clothes, an incision quite three inches long, that had punctured the pillow which lay beneath them—the pillow that had saved him his life—and buried itself in the mattress beneath. Gad! a powerful hand that! He stood a moment thinking, pinching up his chin the while. He had had his suspicions of Borkins, but the face that he had seen in the moonlight was not the butler's face. *Whose, then, was it?*

CHAPTER XIII
A GRUESOME DISCOVERY

Through the long watches of the night Cleek sat there thinking, his chin sunk in one hand, his eyes narrowed down to pin-points, the whole alert personality of the man vitally dominant. No, he would not tell any one of the happening except Dollops and Mr. Narkom. It would only invite suspicion, throw the house into a state of unrest which was the very thing that he was anxious to avoid. As dawn broke, and the danger for that night was past, he got to his feet, plunged his face into cold water, which cleared away the cobwebs, undressed, and then tackled the question of the injured bedding.

The mattress could be turned—that was easy enough, and the slit would probably not be noticed. The bedclothes, too, might be turned the other way up, and with care the injured parts tucked in tightly at the bottom. It would leave them a little short at the top perhaps, but that couldn't be helped. Suspicion must be allayed at all costs. Time enough to bring the would-be murderer to justice when he had solved the riddle in its entirety. There were two pillows, so he took the damaged one, tore off its case, and tucked that away in his kit-bag, pushed the bag under the bed, and then set about the remaking, with some small success. At least for the time, the incisions in the blanket and sheets would not be noticed, and in the morning he would invent some excuse to have them changed.

The early morning cup of tea, brought at eight by a dainty chambermaid in cap and starched blue dress, supplied the need quite nicely. He nodded to her as she left the room, and then, when the door closed, upset the cup on the coverlet, letting the liquid soak through. Then he got up and dressed himself with something like a smile upon his lips.

At breakfast, a housemaid waited upon them, and Cleek ate lustily, with the appetite that is born of good health, and a mind at peace with the world. Toward the end of the meal, however, Borkins came in. He glanced casually over the group at the table, let his eyes rest for a moment upon Cleek, and then—dropped an empty dish he was carrying. As he stooped to recover it, all chance of seeing how the appearance of the man who had so nearly met his death last night affected him, was gone. He came up again still the same, quiet, dignified Borkins of yore. Not a gleam of anything but the most obsequious interest in the task before him marred the tranquillity of his features. If the man knew anything, then he was a fine actor. But—did he? That was the question that interested Cleek during the remainder of the meal.

After it was over, Mr. Narkom and Sir Nigel went off to the smoking room for a quiet cigarette before setting to the real business of the day, and Cleek was left to follow them at his leisure. Borkins was pottering about the table as the two men left the breakfast room, and Cleek stood in the doorway.

"Peaceful night, last night, eh, Borkins?" he said with a slight laugh. "That's the best of this blessed country life of yours. Chap rests so well. Talk about the simple life—" He broke off and laughed again, watching Borkins pick up a clean fork and carry it to the plate-basket upon the sideboard.

The man retained his perfect dignity and ease of manner.

"Quite so, sir. Quite so. I trust you slept well."

"Pretty well—*for a strange bed*," returned Cleek with emphasis, and turned upon his heel. "If you see my man you might send him along to me. I want to arrange with him about suits that are coming down from my tailor's."

"Very good, sir."

Cleek joined the two men with something akin to admiration for the butler's impassiveness in his heart. If he knew anything, then he was a past master in the art of repression. On the other hand perhaps he didn't—and there was really no reason why he should. Eavesdropping was a common enough fault with the best of servants, and curiosity a failing of most men. Borkins might be—and possibly was—absolutely innocent of any knowledge of last night's affair. And yet, how did the knowledge, that he was not altogether what he seemed, leak out? It was a puzzle to which, as yet, Cleek could find no answer.

Mr. Narkom greeted Cleek enthusiastically when he joined him.

"I'm off on a tour of investigation in a few minutes," he announced. "Petrie and Hammond arrived last night, as you know, and are putting up at the village inn. I'm meeting them at the edge of the Fens at ten o'clock. Then we're going to have a good look to see if we can find the bodies of the two men who have vanished. You coming along?"

Cleek nodded, and the queer little one-sided smile travelled up his cheek.

"Certainly, my dear Lake. I'd be delighted. Sir Nigel, of course, has other business to attend to. It's ten minutes to ten now. If you're going you'd better step lively. Ah," as Dollops's figure appeared in the doorway, "if you'll excuse me, Sir Nigel, I'll just have a word or two with my man." His voice dropped several tones as he addressed the boy and they moved away together. "Mr. Lake and I are going out for a walk across the Fens. Petrie and Hammond will be there at ten. I'd like you to join 'em. Better nip along now."

"Yessir."

"And—Dollops"—he beckoned him back and bent his head to the lad's ear, speaking in a voice that none heard but the one it was intended for—"keep a sharp look-out. I had a narrow escape last night. Someone tried to stab me in bed but he got my pillow instead—"

"*Gawdamercy*, Guv'nor!—"

"Ssh. And there's no need to worry. I'm still here, you see. But keep your eyes and your ears open, and if you see any strange men hanging around, report to me at once."

Dollops's usually pale, freckled countenance went a shade paler, and he caught at Cleek's arm as though he were loath to let it go.

"But, sir," he whispered in a hoarse undertone, "you won't go a-knocking about alone, will yer? If anythin' were to 'appen to you—I—I'd go along and commit that there 'harum-scarum' wot the Japanese are so fond o' doin'—on the spot!"

Cleek could barely restrain a laugh. The whispered conversation had taken the merest fraction of a minute and, during it, he had had full view of the green baize door which led down to the servants' quarters. Borkins had gone through it some time before. Then he heard the butler's deep, measured tones in the garden, and caught sight of him talking to one of the grooms in the courtyard. He heaved something like a sigh of relief.

Dollops left, and Cleek then rejoined the two men who stood talking together in low, earnest tones.

"Now," said he, briskly, "if you're ready, Mr. Lake, I am. Let us be off. Sir Nigel, I hope by dinner time to have some sort of news to impart to you, whether good or ill remains to be seen. By the way, have you, in your employ, a dark, square-faced individual, with close-set eyes and a straggling moustache? Rather undershot, too, I believe? It would be interesting to me to know."

Merriton considered for a moment.

"Tell you the truth, Mr. Headland, I can't fit the description in anywhere among the people here," he said after a pause. "Dimmock's fairish—though he *has* got a moustache, but it's a military one, and Borkins is, of course, smooth shaven. The other men are clean-shaved, too, except for old Doughty, the head gardener, and he wears a full, gray beard. Why?"

Cleek shook his head.

"Nothing important. I was only just wondering. Now then, Lake, you'll be late if you loiter any longer, and our—er—friends will be waiting. Good-bye, Sir Nigel, and good luck. Lunch at one-fifteen, I take it?"

He swung upon his heel and linked his arm with Mr. Narkom's, then, taking his cap from a peg on the hall stand, clapped it on his head and went down and out to the task that awaited him, and a discovery which was, to say the least of it, startling in the extreme.

They walked for some time in comparative silence, puffing at their cigarettes. Then of a sudden, Cleek spoke.

"I say, old man, you'll want to keep a close look-out upon your own personal safety," he said, abruptly, wheeling round and meeting his friend full in the eyes.

"What d'you mean, C—Headland?"

"What I say. Someone's got wind of our real purpose here. I have a grave suspicion that that Borkins was listening at my door last evening when I was talking to Dollops. Later—well, somebody or other tried to get me in bed. But I was one too many for him—"

"My dear Cleek!"

"Mr. Lake, I beg of you—not so loud!" ejaculated Cleek. "There are ears everywhere, which you as a policeman ought to know. Do remember my name and don't go losing any sleep over me. I can take care of myself, all right. But I had to do it pretty energetically last night. A thoughtful visitor stabbed the pillow I'd placed in bed instead of my humble self, and cut an incision three inches deep. Hit the mattress, too!"

"Headland, my God—!"

"Now, don't take on so. I tell you I can take care of myself, but you do the same. No one in the house knows a word about it, and

I don't intend that they shall. The less said the better, in a case like this. Only those Frozen Flames are trying to eat up something that is either very serious or very money-making. One thing or the other. … Hello, here we are! Mornin' Petrie; mornin' Hammond. All ready for the search I see."

The two constables, clad in plain clothes and accompanied by Dollops, were holding in their hands long pitchforks which looked more as if they were ready for haymaking than for the gruesome task ahead of them all. Petrie carried upon his arm a roll of rope. They swung into step behind the detectives, across the uneven, marshy ground.

It was a chilly morning, and inclined to rain. Across the flat horizon the mist hung in wraithlike forms of cloudy gray, and the deep grass into which they plunged their feet was beaded with dew. For a time they walked on quietly until they had gone perhaps a quarter of a mile. Then Cleek halted.

"Better separate here," he said, waving his arm out across the sweep of flat country. "Dollops, you take the right with Petrie. Hammond, you'd better try the left. Mr. Narkom and I will go straight ahead together. Any discovery made, just give the usual signal."

They separated at once, their feet upon the thick marshy ground leaving numberless footprints in the moist rank grass, which crushed under them like wet hay. Their heads were bent, their eyes fixed upon the ground, their faces bearing a look of utter concentration. Cleek watched them moving slowly across the wide, flat reaches of the Fens, stopping now and then to poke among the rank marsh-grass, and prod into the earth, and then turned to Mr. Narkom.

"Good fellows—those three," he said with a smile. "What more can you ask than that? Straight ahead for us, Mr. Narkom. Sir Nigel tells me the patch of charred grass lies in a direct line with the edge of the Fens where we started our search. I'm keen to have a look at it."

Mr. Narkom nodded, and walked on, poking here and there with his stout walking stick. Cleek did likewise. They rarely spoke, simply pushed and poked and trod the grass down; searching, searching, searching, as had those other men upon the night of Dacre Wynne's disappearance. But they had searched in vain for any clue which would lead to the elucidation of the mystery.

Suddenly Cleek stopped. He pointed a little ahead of him with his walking stick.

"There you are!" said he briskly. "The patch of charred grass." He strode up to it, stopped and bent his eyes upon it, then suddenly exclaimed: "Look here! Below at the roots the fresh grass is springing up in little tender green shoots. That patch'll disappear shortly. And"—he stopped and sucked in his breath, wheeling round upon Mr. Narkom—"when you come to think of it, why shouldn't it have grown up already? There's been time enough since the man Wynne's disappearance to cover up all those singed ends in a new growth. Can't be that it's done on *purpose*, and yet—why is it still here?"

"Perhaps some sign or something," suggested Mr. Narkom.

"Possibly, something of the sort. And if we have signs then there must be something human behind all this talk of supernatural agents," returned Cleek. "Let us take it that this patch of charred grass *hides* something, or marks the way to something, something buried underneath it, or lying near by. Eh—what's that?"

"That" was a cat-call ringing out across the misty silences from the direction in which Dollops and Petrie had gone.

"They've found something!" cried out Mr. Narkom, in a hoarse whisper of excitement.

"Obviously. Well, this other thing will wait. We'll go after them."

The two of them hastened off in the direction of the repeated cat-call, and soon came upon Dollops bending over something, his eyes rather scared, just as Hammond arrived from the other direction in answer to the summons. Petrie, too, appeared rather nervous. As Cleek came up to them, his eyes fell upon the ground, and he stopped stock still.

"*Gad!*... Where did you find it?"

"Here, sir; half buried, but with the 'ead a-stickin' out!" returned Petrie. "Dollops and I pulled it out and—and 'ere it is."

Cleek glanced down at the body of a heavily built man, clad in evening clothes, and already in an advanced state of decomposition. "Looks like it was that chap Wynne," he said, in a matter-of-fact tone. "Answers the description all right. The other man was short and red-headed. And the evening clothes are well cut from what I can see. Must have been a handsome chap—once. … Well, we'll have to get this very gruesome find back to the Towers as quickly as possible. Got your oilskin with you, Petrie?"

"Yessir!" Petrie miraculously produced the roll from under his tunic and spread the sheet out. Then they lifted up the body and wrapped it about so that the covering hid the awfulness of it from view. Mr. Narkom mopped his forehead with his handkerchief.

"Cinnamon, Cleek!" he ejaculated, breathlessly. "Pretty awful, isn't it? Was it much hidden, Petrie? Funny the other people didn't find it when they searched!"

"No, sir—plain as a pikestaff!" returned Petrie importantly, for he felt the burden of responsibility and hoped that this would mean promotion. Dollops, who was by no means a regular member of the force, simply looked at Cleek with considerable pride fighting through the natural horror that the find had given birth to.

"Funny thing!" broke in Cleek at this juncture. "The only solution must be that the body was placed there some time *after* death. ... Leave it a little longer, boys, and we'll have a further search in this direction. We may come upon poor Collins in a similar fashion—though thank Heaven his disappearance didn't happen quite so long ago."

They took a few steps farther in the same direction and—stopped simultaneously. Before their eyes lay the figure of Collins, in his discreet black clothes, his red head against a tuffet of moss, and a bullet wound in his temple.

"God!" said Cleek, softly, and sucked in his breath. "Two of 'em. And like this!... Looks like a plant, doesn't it? Poor chap!... And yet Merriton declared that he, as well as others, had searched every inch of this ground over and over again. Seems fishy. To find 'em both here—so close together. ... Let's have a look at the other poor chap. ... Hmm. Bullet wound through the right temple, too. Small-calibre revolver."

He bent down and examined the head carefully through his magnifying glass, then got slowly to his feet.

"Well, Mr. Narkom," said he, steadily, "nothing to be done at present, but to get these bodies back to the Towers. After that they can take 'em to the village mortuary if they like. But I've one or two things I'd like to ask you Merriton, and one or two things I want to examine. Gad! it's a beastly task, boys. That sheet's big enough, thank fortune! Cross the pitchforks, Petrie, and make a sort of stretcher out of them, that way. That's right. Now then, forward. ... Gad! *what* a morning!"

But if he had known just exactly what the rest of that morning was to bring forth, indeed before lunch was served at one-fifteen, he might have hesitated to pass judgment upon it so soon.

Slowly the cavalcade wended its way across the rank grass. …

CHAPTER XIV

THE SPIN OF THE WHEEL

Merriton stood at the study window, looking out, and pulling at his cigar with an air of profound meditation. Upon the hearth-rug Doctor Bartholomew, clad in baggy tweeds, stood tugging at his beard and watched the man's back with kindly, troubled eyes.

"Don't like it, Nigel, my boy; don't like it at all!" he ejaculated, suddenly, in his close-clipped fashion. "These detectives are the very devil to pay. Get 'em in one's house and they're like doctors—including, of course, my humble self—difficult to get out. Part of the profession, my boy. But a beastly nuisance. Seems to me I'd rather have the mystery than the men. Simpler, anyway. And fees, you know, are heavy."

Merriton swung round upon his heel suddenly, his brows like a thunder cloud.

"I don't care a damn about that," he broke out angrily. "Let 'em take every penny I've got, so long as they solve the thing! But I can't get away from it—I just can't. Hangs over me night and day like the sword of Damocles! Until the mystery of Wynne's disappearance is cleared up, I tell you 'Toinette and I can't marry. She feels the same. And—and—we've the house all ready, you know, everything fixed and in order, except *this*. When poor old Collins disappeared, too, I found I'd reached my limit. So here these detectives are, and, on the whole, jolly decent chaps I find 'em."

Doctor Bartholomew shrugged his shoulders as if to say, "Have it your own way, my boy." But what he really *did* say was:

"What are their names?"

"Young chap's Headland—George or John Headland, I don't remember quite which. Other one's Lake—Gregory Lake."

"H'm. Good name that, Nigel. Ought to be some brains behind it. But I never did pin my faith on policemen, you know, boy. Scotland Yard's made so many mistakes that if it hadn't been for that chap Cleek, they'd have ruined themselves altogether. Now, he's a man, if you like! Pity you couldn't get *him* while you're about it."

The impulse to tell who "George Headland" really was to this firm friend who had been more than a father to him, even in the old days, and who had made a point of dropping down upon him, informally, ever since the trouble over Dacre Wynne's disappearance, took hold of Nigel. But he shook it off. He had given his word. And if he could not tell 'Toinette, then no other soul in the universe should know. So he simply tossed his shoulders, and, going back to the window, looked out of it, to hide the something of triumph which had stolen into his face.

Truth to tell, he was obsessed with a feeling that something *was* going to happen, and happen soon. The premonition, to one who was not used to such things, carried all the more conviction. With Cleek on the track—anything might happen. Cleek was a man for whom things never stood still, and his amazing brain was concentrated upon this problem as it had been concentrated—successfully—upon others. Merriton had a feeling that it was only a matter of time.

Then, just as he was standing there, humming something softly beneath his breath, the cavalcade, headed by Cleek and Mr. Narkom, rather grim and silent, reached the gateway. Behind them—Merriton gave a sudden cry which brought the doctor to his side—behind them three men were carrying something—something bulky and large and wrapped in a black oilskin tarpaulin. And one of the men was Headland's servant, Dollops! He recognized that, even as his inner consciousness told him that his "something" was about to happen now.

"Gad! they've found the body," he exclaimed, in a hoarse, excited voice, fairly running to the front door and throwing it open with a crash that rang through the old house from floor to rafters, and brought Borkins scuttling up the kitchen stairs at a pace that was ill-befitting his age and dignity. Merriton gave him a curt order.

"Have the morning-room door thrown open and the sofa pulled out from against the wall. My friends have been for a walk across the Fens, and have found something. You can see them coming up the drive. What d'you make of it?"

"Gawd! a haccident, Sir Nigel," said Borkins, in a shaky voice. "'Adn't I better tell Mrs. Mummery to put the blue bedroom in order and 'ave plenty of 'ot water? … "

"No." Merriton was running down the front steps and flung the answer back over his shoulder. "Can't you use your eyes? It's a body, you fool—a body!"

Borkins gasped a moment, and then stood still, his thin lips sucked in, his face unpleasant to see. He was alone in the hallway, for Doctor Bartholomew's fat figure was waddling in Merriton's wake.

He put up his fist and shook it in their direction.

"Pity it ain't your body, young upstart that you are!" he muttered beneath his breath, and turned toward the morning room.

Meanwhile Merriton had reached the solemn little party and was walking back beside Cleek, his face chalky, the pupils of his eyes a trifle dilated with excitement.

"Found 'em? Found 'em *both*, you say, Mr. Headland?" he kept on repeating over and over again, as they mounted the steps together. "Good God! What a strange—what a peculiar thing! I'll swear there was no sight nor sign of them when I've tramped over the Fens dozens of times. I don't know what to make of it, I don't indeed!"

"Oh, we'll make something of it all right," returned Cleek, with a sharp look at him, for there was one thing he wanted to find out, and he meant to do that as soon as possible. "Two and two, you know, put together properly, always make four. It's only the fools of the world that add wrong. If you'd had as much practice as I've had in dealing with humanity, you'd find it was an ever-increasing astonishment to see the way things dovetail in. ... Who's this, by the way?"

He jerked his head in the direction of the doctor, who had stopped at the foot of the steps and waited for them to come up to him.

"Oh, a very old friend of mine, Mr. Headland. Doctor Bartholomew. Has a very big practice in town, but a trifle eccentric, as you can see at first glance."

Cleek sent his keen eyes over the odd-looking figure in the worn tweeds.

"I see. Then can you tell me how he finds time to run down here at leisure and visit you? Seems to me a man with a big practice never has enough time to work it in. At least, that has been my experience of doctors."

Merriton flushed angrily at the tone. He whipped his head round and met Cleek's cool gaze hotly.

"I know you're down here to investigate the case, but I don't think there's any reason for you to start suspecting my friends," he retorted, his eyes flashing. "Doctor Bartholomew has a partner, if you want to know. And also he's supposed to be retired. But he carries on for the love of the thing. Best man ever breathed—remember that!"

Cleek smiled to himself at the sudden onslaught. The young

pepper-pot! Yet he liked him for the loyal defence of his friend, never-theless. There were all too few creatures in the world who found it impossible to suspect those whom they cared for, and who cared for them.

"Sorry to have given any offence, I'm sure," he said, smoothly. "None was meant, right enough, Sir Nigel. But a policeman has an unpleasant duty, you know. He's got to keep his eyes and his ears open. So if you find mine open too far, any time, just tip me the wink and I'll shut 'em up again."

"Oh, that's all right," said Merriton, mollified, and a trifle shame-faced at the outburst. Then, with an effort to turn the conversation: "But think of findin' 'em both, Mr.—er—Headland! Were they—very awful?"

"Pretty awful," returned Cleek, quietly; "eh, Mr. Lake?"

"God bless my soul—*yes!*" threw in that gentleman, with a shudder. "Now then, boys, if you don't mind—" He took the attitude of a casual acquaintance with his two assistants who helped to bear the burden. "Come along inside. This way—that's it. Where did you say, Merriton? Into the morning room? All right. Ah, Borkins has been getting things ready, I see. That couch is a broad one. Good thing, as there are two of 'em."

"*Two* of 'em, sir?" exclaimed Borkins, suddenly throwing up his hands, his eyes wide with horror. Mr. Narkom nodded with some-thing of professional triumph in his look.

"Two of 'em, Borkins. And the second one, if I don't make any mistake, answers to the description of James Collins—eh, Headland?"

Cleek gave him a sudden look that spoke volumes. It came over him in a flash that Narkom had said too much; that it wasn't the casual visitor's place to know what a servant who was not there at the time of his visit looked like.

"At least—that's as far as I can make out from what Sir Nigel told me of him the other day," he supplemented, in an effort to make amends. "Now then, boys, put 'em there on the couch. Poor things! I warn you, Sir Nigel, this isn't going to be a pleasant sight, but you've got to go through with it, I'm afraid. The police'll want identification made, of course. Hadn't you better 'phone the local branch? Someone ought to be here in charge, you know."

Merriton nodded. He was so stunned at the actuality of these two men's deaths, at the knowledge that their bodies—lifeless, extinct—

were here in his morning room, that he had stood like an image, making no move, no sound.

"Yes—yes," he said, rapidly, waving a hand in Borkins's direction. "See that it's done at once, please. Tell Constable Roberts to come along with a couple of his men. Very decent of these chaps to give you a hand, Mr. Lake. That's your man, Dollops, isn't it, Headland? Well, hadn't he better take 'em downstairs and give 'em a stiff whisky-and-soda? I expect the poor beggars have need of it."

Cleek held up a silencing hand.

"No," he said, firmly. "Not just yet, I think. They may be needed for evidence when the constable comes. Now. ..." He crossed over to where the bodies lay, and gently removed the covering. Merriton went suddenly white, while the doctor, more used to such sights, bit his lips and laid a steadying hand upon the younger man's arm.

"My God!" cried Sir Nigel, despairingly. "How did they meet their death?"

Cleek reached down a finger and gently touched a blackened spot upon Wynne's temple.

"Shot through the head, and the bullet penetrated the brain," he said, quietly. "Small-calibre revolver, too. There's your Frozen Flame for you, my friend!"

But he was hardly prepared for the event that followed. For at this statement, Merriton threw a hand out suddenly, as though warding off a blow, took a step forward and peered at that which had once been his friend—and enemy—and then gave out a strangled cry.

"Shot through the head!" he fairly shrieked, as Borkins came quietly into the room, and stopped short at the sound of his master's voice. "I tell you it's impossible—*impossible*! It wasn't my shot, Mr. Headland—it couldn't have been!"

CHAPTER XV

A STARTLING DISCLOSURE

Cleek took a sudden step forward.

"What's that? What's that?" he rapped out, sharply. "*Your* shot, Sir Nigel? This is something I haven't heard of before, and it's likely to cause trouble. Explain, please!"

But Merriton was past explaining anything just then. For he had bowed his head in his hands and was sobbing in great, heart-wrung sobs with Doctor Bartholomew's arms about him, sobs that told of the nerve-strain which gave them birth, that told of the tenseness under which he had lived these last weeks. And now the thread had snapped, and all the broken, jangling nerves of the man had been loosed and torn his control to atoms.

The doctor shook him gently, but with firm fingers.

"Don't be a fool, boy—don't be a fool!" he said over and over again, as he waved the other away, and, taking out a little phial from his waistcoat pocket, dropped a dose from it into a wine-glass and forced it between the man's lips. "Don't make an ass of yourself, Nigel. The shot you fired was nothing—the mere whim of a man, whose brain had been fired by champagne and who wasn't therefore altogether responsible for his actions."

He whipped round suddenly upon Cleek, his faded eyes, with their fringe of almost white lashes, flashing like points of light from the seamed and wrinkled frame of his face.

"If you want to hear that foolish part of the story, I can give it to you," he said, sharply. "Because I happened to be there."

"*You!*"

"Yes—I, Mr.—er—Headland, isn't it? Ah, thanks. But the boy's unstrung, nerve-racked. He's been through too much. The whole beastly thing has made a mess of him, and he was a fool to meddle with it. Nigel Merriton fired a shot that night when Dacre Wynne disappeared, Mr. Headland; fired it after he had gone up to his room, a little over-excited with too much champagne, a little over-wrought by the scene through which he had just passed with the man who had always exercised such a sinister influence over his life."

"So Sir Nigel was no good friend of this man Wynne's, then?"

remarked Cleek, quietly, as if he did not already know the fact.

The doctor looked up as though he were ready to spring upon him and tear him limb from limb.

"No!" he said, furiously, "and neither would you have been, if you'd known him. Great hulking bully that he was! I tell you, I've seen the man use his influence upon this boy here, until—fine, upstanding chap that he is (and I've known him and his people ever since he was a baby) he succeeded in making him as weak as a hysterical girl— and gloated over it, too!"

Cleek drew in a quiet breath, and gave his shoulders the very slightest of twitches, to show that he was listening.

"Very interesting, Doctor, as psychological studies of the kind go," he said, smoothly, stroking his chin and looking down at the bowed shoulders of the man in the arm chair, with something almost like sorrow in his eyes. "But we've got to get down to brass tacks, you know. This thing's serious. It's got to be proved. If it can't be— well, it's going to be mighty awkward for Sir Nigel. Now, let's hear the thing straight out from the person most interested, please. I don't like to appear thoughtless in any way, but this is a serious admission you've just made. Sir Nigel, I beg of you, tell us the story before the constable comes. It might make things easier for you in the long run."

Merriton, thus addressed, threw up his head suddenly and showed a face marked with mental anguish, dry-eyed, deathly white. He got slowly to his feet and went over to the table, leaning his hand upon it as though for support.

"Oh, well," he said, listlessly, "you might as well hear it first as last. Doctor Bartholomew's right, Mr. Headland. I *did* fire a shot upon the night of Dacre Wynne's disappearance, and I fired it from my bedroom window. It was like this:

"Wynne had gone, and after waiting for him to come back away past the given time, we all made up our minds to go to bed, and Tony West—a pal of mine who was one of the guests—and the Doctor here accompanied me to my room door. Dr. Bartholomew had a room next to mine. In that part of the house the walls are thin, and although my revolver (which I always carry with me, Mr. Headland, since I lived in India) is one of those almost soundless little things, still, the sound of it reached him."

"Is it of small calibre?" asked Cleek, at this juncture.

Merriton nodded gravely.

"As you say, of small calibre. You can see it for yourself. Borkins"—he turned toward the man, who was standing by the doorway, his hands hanging at his sides, his manner a trifle obsequious; "will you bring it from the left-hand drawer of my dressing table. Here is the key." He tossed over a bunch of keys and they fell with a jangling sound upon the floor at Borkins's feet.

"Very good, Sir Nigel," said the man and withdrew, leaving the door open behind him, however, as though he were afraid to lose any of the story that was being told in the quiet morning room.

When he had gone, Merriton resumed:

"I'm not a superstitious man, Mr. Headland, but that old wives' tale of the Frozen Flames, and the new one coming out every time they claimed another victim, seemed to have burnt its way into my brain. That and the champagne together, and then close upon it Dacre Wynne's foolish bet to find out what the things were. When I went up to my room, and after saying good-night to the doctor here, closed the door and locked it, I then crossed to the window and looked out at the flames. And as I looked—believe it or not, as you will—another flame suddenly sprang up at the left of the others, a flame that seemed brighter, bigger than any of the rest, a flame that bore with it the message: 'I am Dacre Wynne'."

Cleek smiled, crookedly, and went on stroking his chin.

"Rather a fanciful story that, Sir Nigel," he said, "but go on. What happened?"

"Why, I fired at the thing. I picked up my revolver and, in a sort of blind rage, fired at it through the open window; and I believe I said something like this: 'Damn it, why won't you go? I'll make you go, you maddening little devil!' though I know those weren't the identical words I spoke. As soon as the shot was fired my brain cleared. I began to feel ashamed of myself, thought what a fool I'd look in front of the boys if they heard the story; and just at that moment Doctor Bartholomew knocked at the door."

Here the doctor nodded vigorously as thought to corroborate these statements, and made as if to speak.

Cleek silenced him with a gesture.

"And then—what next, Sir Nigel?"

Merriton cleared his throat before proceeding. There was a drawn look upon his face.

"The doctor said he thought he had heard a shot, and asked me what it was, and I replied: 'Nothing. Only I was potting at the flames.' This seemed to amaze him, as it would any sane man, I should think, and as no doubt it is amazing you, Mr. Headland. Amazing you and making you think, 'What a fool the fellow is, after all!' Well, I showed the doctor the revolver in my hand, and he laughingly said that he'd take it to bed with him, in case I should start potting at *him* by mistake. Then I got into bed, after making him promise he wouldn't breathe a word to anybody of what had occurred, as the others would be sure to laugh at me; and—that's all."

"H'm. And quite enough, too, I should say," broke in Cleek, as the man finished. "It sounds true enough, believe me, from your lips, and I know you for an honourable man; but—what sort of a credence do you think an average jury is going to place upon it? D'you think they'd believe you?" He shook his head. "Never. They'd simply laugh at the whole thing, and say you were either drunk or dreaming. People in the twentieth century don't indulge in superstition to that extent, Sir Nigel; or, at least, if they do, they let their reason govern their actions as far as possible. It's a tall story at best, if you'll forgive me for saying so."

Merriton's face went a dull, sultry red. His eyes flamed.

"Then you don't believe me?" he said, impatiently.

Cleek raised a hand.

"I don't say that for one moment," he replied. "What I say is: 'Would a judge and jury believe you?' That is the question. And my answer to it is, 'No.' You've had every provocation to take Dacre Wynne's life, so far as I can learn, every provocation, that is, that a man of unsound mentality who would stoop to murder could have to justify himself in his own eyes. Things look exceedingly black against you, Sir Nigel. You can swear to this statement as far as your part in it is concerned, Doctor Bartholomew?"

"Absolutely," said the doctor, though plainly showing that he felt it was no business of the supposed Mr. Headland's.

"Well, that's good. But if only there had been another witness, someone who actually saw this thing done, or who had heard the pistol-shot—not that I'm doubting your word at all, Doctor—it might help to elucidate matters. There is no one you know of who could have heard—and not spoken?"

At this juncture Borkins came quietly into the room, holding the little revolver in his right hand, and handed it to Cleek.

"If you please, sir," he said, impassively, and with a quick look into Merriton's grave face, "*I* heard. And I can speak, if the jury wants me to, I don't doubt but what my tale would be worth listenin' to, if only to add my hevidence to the rest. That man there"—he pointed one shaking forefinger at his master's face, and glowered into it for a moment "was the murderer of poor Mr. Wynne!"

CHAPTER XVI

TRAPPED!

"You damned, skulking liar!"

Merriton leapt forward suddenly, and it was with difficulty that Cleek could restrain him from seizing the butler round the throat.

"Gently, gently, my friend," interposed Cleek, as he neatly caught Merriton's upthrown arm. "It won't help you, you know, to attack a possible witness. We've got to hear what this man says, to know whether he's speaking the truth or not—and we've got to go into his evidence as clearly as we go into yours. ... You're perfectly right, Doctor, I *am* a policeman, and I'm down here for the express purpose of investigating this appalling affair. The expression of your face so plainly said, 'What right has he to go meddling in another man's affairs like this?' that I was obliged to confess the fact, for the sake of my self-respect. My friend here, Mr. Lake, is working with me." At this he gave Borkins a keen, searching look, and saw in the man's impassive countenance that this was no news to him. "Now then, my man, speak out. You tell us you heard that revolver-shot when your master fired it from his bedroom. Where are your quarters?"

"On the other side of the 'ouse, sir," returned Borkins, flushing a trifle. "But I was up in me dressing gown, as I'd some'ow thought that something was amiss. I'd 'eard the quarrel that 'ad taken place between Sir Nigel and poor Mr. Wynne, and I'd 'eard 'im go out and slam the door be'ind 'im. So I was keeping me ears peeled, as you might say."

"I see. Doing a bit of eavesdropping, eh?" asked Cleek, and was rewarded by an angry look from under the man's dark brows and a sudden tightening of the lines about his mouth. "And what then?"

"I kept about, first in the bathroom, and then in the 'all, keeping my ears open, for I'd an idea that one day things would come to a 'ead between 'em. Sir Nigel had taken Mr. Wynne's girl and—"

"Close your lying mouth, you vile beast!" spat out Merriton, vehemently, "and don't you dare to mention her name, or I'll stop you for ever from speaking, whether I hang or not!"

Borkins looked at Cleek, and his look quite plainly conveyed the meaning that he wished the detective to notice how violent Sir Nigel could be on occasions, but if Cleek saw this he paid not the slightest heed.

"Speak as briefly as you can, please, and give as little offence," he cut in, in a sharp tone, and Borkins resumed:

"At last I saw Sir Nigel and the Doctor and Mr. West come up the corridor together. I 'eard 'em bid each other good-night, saw the Doctor go into 'is room, and Mr. West return to the smoking-room, and 'eard Sir Nigel's key turn in 'is lock. After that there was silence for a bit, and all I 'ears was 'is moving about and muttering to 'imself, as though 'e was angry about something. Then, just as I was a-goin' back to me own room, I 'eard the pistol-shot, and nips back again. I 'eard 'im say, 'Got you—you devil!' and then without waitin' for anything else, I runs down to the servants' 'all, which is directly below the smoking room where the other gentlemen were talking and smoking. I peers out of the window, upward—for it's a half-basement, as perhaps you've noticed, sir—and there, in the light of the moon, I see Mr. Wynne's figure, crouched down against the gravel of the front path, and makin' funny sorts of noises. And then, all of a sudden, 'e went still as a dead man—and 'e *was* a dead man. With that I flies to me own room, frightened half out of me wits—for I'm a peace-lovin' person, and easily scared, I'm afraid—and then I locks meself in, sayin' over and over to meself the words, 'He's done it! He's done it at last! He's murdered Mr. Wynne, he has!' And that's all I 'ave to say, sir."

"And a damned sight too much, too, you liar!" threw in Merriton, furiously, his face convulsed with passion, the veins on his temple standing out like whipcords. "Why, the whole story's a fake. And if it *were* true, tell me how I could get Wynne's body out of the way so quickly, and without any one hearing me, when every man in that smoking room, from their own words, and from those of the doctor here, was at that moment straining his ears for any possible sound? The smoking room flanks straight on the drive, Mr.—er—Headland—" He caught himself up just in time as he saw Cleek's almost impercep-tible signal, and then went on, his voice gaining in strength and fury with every word: "I'm not a giant, am I? I couldn't have lifted Wynne *alive* and with his own assistance, much less lift him dead when he'd be a good sight heavier. Why, the thing's a tissue of lies, I tell you—a beastly, underhanded, backbiting tissue of lies, and if ever I get out of this thing alive, I'll show Borkins exactly what I think of him. And why you should give credence to the story of a lying servant, rather than to mine, I cannot see at all. Would I have brought you here, you, a man whose name—" And even in the excitement which had him in its grip Nigel felt Cleek's will, powerful, compelling, preventing his giving away the secret of his identity, preventing his telling that it was the master mind among the criminal investigators of Europe which was working on this horrible affair.

He went on, still in a fury of indignation, but with the knowledge of Mr. Headland's true name still locked in his breast. "Did I bring you here as a friend and give you every opportunity to work on this strange business, to have you arraign me as a murderer? Do not treat me as a suspect, Mr. Detective. I am not on trial. I want this thing cleared up, yes; but I am not here to be accused of the murder of a man who was a guest in my own house, by the very man I brought in to find the true murderer."

"You haven't given me time to say whether I accuse you or not, Sir Nigel," replied Cleek, patiently. "Now, if you'll permit me to speak, we'll take up this man's evidence. There are gaps in it that rather badly want filling up, and there are thin places which I hardly think would hold water before a judge and jury. But he swears himself a witness, and there you are. And as for believing his word before yours—who fired the shot, Sir Nigel? Did he, or did you? I am a representative of the Law and as such I entered your house."

Merriton made no reply, simply held his head a little higher and clasped the edge of the table more firmly.

"Now," said Cleek, turning to the butler and fixing him with his keen eyes. "You are ready to swear that this is true, upon your oath, and knowing that perjury is punishable by law?"

"Yes, sir." Borkins's voice was very low and rather indistinct.

"Very well. Then may I ask why you did not immediately report this matter to the rest of the party, or to the police?"

Something flashed across Borkins's face, and was gone again. He cleared his throat nervously before replying:

"I felt on me honour to—Sir Nigel, sir," he returned at length. "A man stands by his master, you know—if 'e's a good one; and though we'd 'ad words before, I didn't bear 'im no malice. And I didn't want the old 'ouse to come to disgrace."

"So you waited until things looked a little blacker for him, and then decided to cast your creditable scruples to the wind?" said Cleek, the queer little one-sided smile travelling up his cheek. "I take it that you had had what you term 'words' since that fatal date?"

Borkins nodded. He did not like this cross-examination, and his nervousness was apparent in voice and look and action.

"Yes, sir."

"II'm. And if we put that to one side altogether can you give me any reason why I should believe this unlikely story in place of the equally unlikely one that your master has told me—knowing what I do?"

Borkins twitched up his head suddenly, his eyes fear-filled, his face turned suddenly gray.

"I—I—What can you know about me, but that I 'ave been in the employment of this family nearly all my life?" he returned, taken off his guard by Cleek's remark. "I'm only a poor, honest workin' man, sir, been in the same place nigh on to twenty years and—"

"And hoping you can hang on another twenty, I dare say!" threw in Cleek, sarcastically. "Oh, I know more about you, my man, than I care to tell. But at the moment that doesn't enter into the matter. We'll take that up later. Now then, there's the revolver. Doctor, you should be useful here; if you will use your professional skill in the service of the law that seems trying to embroil your friend. I want you to examine the head wound, please—the head wound of the man called Dacre Wynne, and, if you can, remove the bullet that is lodged in the brain. Then we shall have a chance to compare it with those remaining in Sir Nigel's revolver."

"I—can't do it, Mr. Headland," returned Doctor Bartholomew, firmly. "I won't lend myself to a plot to inveigle this poor boy, to ruin his life—"

"And I demand it—in the name of the Law." He motioned to Petrie and Hammond, who through the whole length of the inquiry had stood with Dollops, beside the doorway. They came forward swiftly. "Arrest Doctor Bartholomew for treating the Law with contempt—"

"But, I say, Mr. Headland, this is a damned outrage!"

Cleek held up a hand.

"Yes," he said, "I agree with you. But a very necessary one. Besides"—he smiled suddenly into the seamed, anxious face of the man—"who knows but that bullet may prove Sir Nigel's innocence? Who knows but that it is not the same kind as lie now in this deadly little thing here in my hand? It lies with you, Doctor. Must I arrest him now, and take him off to the public jail to await trial, or will you give him a sporting chance?"

The doctor looked up into the keen eyes bent upon him, his own equally keen. He did not know whether he liked this man of the law or not. Something of the man's personality, unfortunate as had been its revelation during this past trying hour, had caught him in its thrall. He measured him, eye for eye, but Cleek's never wavered.

"I've no instruments," he said at last, hedging for time.

"I have plenty—upstairs. I have dabbled a little in surgery myself, when occasion has arisen. I'll fetch them in a minute. You will?"

The doctor stood up between the two tall policemen who had a hand upon either shoulder. His face was set like a mask.

"It's a damned outrage, but I will," he said.

Dollops was gone like a flash. In the meantime Cleek cleared the room. He sent Merriton off to the smoking room in charge of Petrie and Hammond, and Borkins with them—though Borkins was to be kept in the hallway, away from his master's touch and voice.

Cleek, Mr. Narkom, and the doctor remained alone in the room of death, where the doctor set to his gruesome task. Outside, Constable Roberts's burly voice could be heard holding forth in the hall upon the fact that he'd been after a poacher on Mr. Jimmeson's estate over to Saltfleet, and wasn't in when they came for him.

And the operation went quietly on. ...

... In the smoking room, with Hammond and Petrie seated like deaf mutes upon either side of him, Merriton reviewed the whole awful affair from start to finish, and felt his heart sink like lead in his breast. Oh, what a fool he had been to have these men down here! What a fool! To see them wilfully trumping up a charge of murder against himself was—well, it was enough to make any sane man lose hold on his reason. And 'Toinette! His little 'Toinette! If he should be convicted and sent to prison, what would become of her? It would break her heart. And he might never see her again! A sudden moisture pricked at the corners of his eyes. God!—never to call her *wife*!... How long were those beasts going to brood in there over the dead? And was there not a chance that the bullet might be different? After all, wasn't it almost impossible that the bullet *should* be the same? His was an unusual little revolver made by a firm in French Africa, having a different sort of cartridge. Every Tom, Dick, and Harry didn't have one—couldn't afford it, in the first place. ... There was a chance—yes, certainly there was a *chance*.

… His blood began to hammer in his veins again, and his heart beat rapidly. Hope went through him like wine, drowning all the fears and terrors that had stalked before him like demons from another world. He heard, with throbbing pulses, approaching footsteps in the hall. His head was swimming, his feet seemed loaded with lead so that he could not rise. Then, across the space from where Cleek stood, the revolver in one hand and the tiny black object that had nested in a dead man's brain in the other, came the sound of his voice, speaking in clear, concise sentences. He could see the doctor's grave face over the curve of Mr. Narkom's fat shoulder. For a moment the world swam. Then he caught the import of what Cleek was saying.

"The bullet is the same as those in your revolver, Sir Nigel," he said, concisely. "I am sorry, but I must do my duty. Constable Roberts, here is your prisoner. I arrest this man for the murder of Dacre Wynne!"

CHAPTER XVII

IN THE CELL

What followed was like a sort of nightmare to Merriton. That he should be arrested for the murder of Dacre Wynne reeled drunkenly in his brain. Murderer! They were calling him a murderer! The liars! The fools! Calling him a murderer, were they? And taking the word of a crawling worm like Borkins, a man without honour and utterly devoid of decency, who could stand up before them and tell them a story that was a tissue of lies. It was appalling! What a fiend incarnate this man Cleek was! Coming here at Nigel's own bidding, and then suddenly manipulating the evidence, until it caught him up in its writhing coils like a well-thrown lasso. Oh, if he had only let well enough alone and not brought a detective to the house. Yet how was he to know that the man would try to fix a murder on him, himself? Useless for him to speak, to deny. The revolver-shot and the cruel little bullet (which showed there were others who possessed that sort of fire-arm besides himself) proved too easily, upon the circumstantial evidence theory at all events, that his word was naught.

He went through the next hour or two like a man who has been tortured. Silent, but bearing the mark of it upon his white face and in his haggard eyes. And indeed his situation was a terrible and strange one. He had set the wheels of the law in motion; he himself had brought the relentless Hamilton Cleek into the affair and now he was called a murderer!

In the little cell where they placed him, away from the gaping, murmuring, gesticulating knot of villagers that had marked his progress to the police-station—for news flies fast in the country, especially when there is a viper-tongue like Borkins's to wing it on its way—he was thankful for the momentary peace and quiet that the place afforded. At least he could *think*—think and pace up and down the narrow room with its tiny barred window too high for a man to reach, and its hard camp bedstead with the straw mattress, and go through the whole miserable fabrication that had landed him there.

The second day of confinement brought him a visitor. It was 'Toinette. His jailer—a rough-haired village-hand who had taken up with the "Force" and wore the uniform as though it belonged to someone else (which indeed it had)—brought him news of her arrival. It cut him like a lash to see her thus, and yet the longing for her was so great that it superseded all else. So he faced the man with a grim smile.

"I suppose, Bennett, that I shall be allowed to see Miss Brellier? You have made enquiries?"

"Yes, sir." Bennett was crestfallen and rather ashamed of his duty.

"Any restrictions?"

Bennett hedged.

"Well—if you please—Sir Nigel—that is—"

"What the devil are they, then?"

"Constable Roberts give orders that I was to stay 'ere with you—but I can turn me back," returned Bennett, with flushing countenance. "Shall I show the lady in?"

"Yes."

She came. Her frock was of some clinging gray material that made her look more fairy-like than ever. A drooping veil of gray gauze fell like a mist before her face, screening from him the anguished mirrors of her eyes.

"Nigel! My poor, poor Nigel!"

"Little 'Toinette!"

"Oh, Nigel—it seems impossible—utterly! That you should be thought to have killed Dacre. You of all people! Poor, peace-loving Nigel! Something must be done, dearest; something *shall* be done! You shall not suffer so, for someone else's sin—you shall not!"

He smiled at her wanly, and told her how beautiful she was. It was useless to explain to her the utter futility of it all. There was the revolver and there the bullet. The weapon was his—of the bullet he could say nothing. He had only told the truth—and they had not believed him.

"Yes see, dear," he said, patiently, "they do not believe me. They say I killed him, and Borkins—lying devil that he is—has told them a story of how the thing was done; sworn, in fact, that he saw it all from the kitchen window, saw Wynne lying in the garden path, dying, after I fired at him. Of course the thing's an outrageous lie, but—they're acting upon it."

"*Nigel!* How dared he?"

"Who? Borkins? That kind of a devil dares anything. … How's your uncle, dear? He has heard, of course?"

Her face brightened, her eyes were suddenly moist. She put her hands upon his shoulders and tilted her chin so that she could see his eyes.

"Uncle Gustave told me to tell you that he does not believe a word of it, dearest!" she said, softly. "And he is going to make investigations himself. He is so unhappy, so terribly unhappy over it all. Such a tangled web as it is, such a wicked, wicked plot they have woven about you! Oh, Nigel dearest—*why* did you not tell me that they were detectives, these friends of yours who were coming to visit? If you had only said—"

He held her a moment, and then, leaning forward, kissed her gently upon the forehead.

"What then, *p'tite*?"

"I would have made you send them away—I would! I would!" she cried, vehemently. "They should not have come—not if I had wired to them myself! Something told me that day, after you were gone, that a dreadful thing would happen. I was frightened for you—frightened! And I could not tell why! I kept laughing at myself, trying to tease myself out of it, as though it were simply—what you call it?—the 'blues'. And now—this!"

He nodded.

"And now—this," he said, grimly, and laughed.

Bennett, hand upon watch, turned apologetically at this juncture.

"Sorry, Sir Nigel," he said, "but time's up. Ten minutes is the time allowed a prisoner, and—and—I'm afeared the young leddy must go. It 'urts me to tell you, sir, but—you'll understand. Dooty is dooty."

"Yes, doubtless, Bennett, though some people's idea of it is different from others'," returned Merriton, with a bleak smile. "Have no fear, 'Toinette. There is still plenty of time, and I shall engage the finest counsel in the land to stand for me. This knot shall be broken somehow, this tissue of lies must have a flaw somewhere. And nowadays circumstantial evidence, you know, doesn't hold too much water in a court of law. God bless you, little 'Toinette."

She clung to him a moment, her face suddenly lightening at the tenor of his words—so bravely spoken, with so little conviction behind them. But they had helped her, and for that he was glad.

When she had gone, he sat down on the edge of his narrow bed and dropped his face in the cup of his hands. How hopeless it seemed. What chance had he of a future now—with Cleek against him? Cleek the unraveller of a thousand riddles that had puzzled the cleverest brains in the universe! Cleek would never admit to having made a blunder this time—though there was a sort of grim satisfaction in the knowledge that he *had* blundered, though he himself was the victim.

… He sat there for a long time, thinking, his brain wearied, his heart like lead. Bennett's heavily-booted feet upon the stone floor brought him back again to realities.

"There's another visitor, sir," said he. "A gentleman. Seen 'im up at the Towers, I 'ave. Name of West, sir. Constable Roberts says as 'ow you may see him."

How kind of the constable, thought Nigel bitterly. His mouth twisted into a wry smile. Then his eyes lightened suddenly. Tony West, eh? So all the rats hadn't deserted the sinking ship, after all. There were still the old doctor, who came, cheering him up with kind words, bringing him books that he thought he could read—as though a man *could* read books, under such circumstances—and now Tony West—good old West!

West strode in, his five-feet-three of manhood looking as though it were ready to throw the jailer's six-feet-one out of the window upon request, and seized Nigel's hand, wringing it furiously.

"Good old Nigel! Gad! but it's fine to see you. And what fool put you in this idiotic predicament? Wring his damned neck, I would. How are you, old sport?"

Under such light badinage did West try to conceal his real feeling but there was a tremour of the lips that spoke so banteringly.

Good old West! A friend in a thousand.

"Nice sort of place for the Squire of the Manor to be disporting himself, isn't it?" returned Merriton, fighting his hardest to keep his composure and reply in the same light tone. "I—I—damn it, Tony, you don't believe it, do you?"

West went red to the rim of his collar. He choked with the vehemence of his response.

"Believe it, man? D'you think I'm crazy? What sort of a fool would I be to believe it? Wasn't I there, that night, with you? Wait until I give my evidence in court. Bullet or no bullet, you're no—no murderer, Nigel; I'd swear my life away on that. There were others on worse terms with Wynne than you, old chap. There was Stark, for one. Stark used to borrow money from him in the old days, you know, until they had a devil of a shindy over an I.O.U. and the friendship bust. You'd no more reason to kill him than Lester Stark, I swear. Or me, for that matter."

"No, I'd no reason to kill him, Tony. But they'll take that quarrel we had over the Frozen Flame that night, and bring it up against me in court. They'll bring everything against me; everything that can be twisted or turned or bullied into blackening my name. If ever I get scot-free, I'll kill that man Borkins."

West put up his hand suddenly.

"Don't," he said, quietly; "or they'll be putting that against you, too. Believe me, Nigel, old boy, the Law's the greatest duffer on earth. By the way, here's a piece of news for you! Heard it as I stopped in at the Towers this morning. Saw that man Headland, the detective. He told me to tell you, and I clean forgot. But they found an I.O.U. on Wynne's body, an I.O.U. for two thou'—in Lester Stark's name. Dated two nights before the party. Looks a bit funny, that, doesn't it?"

Funny? Merriton felt his heart suddenly bound upward, and as suddenly drop back in his breast like lead. Glad that there was a chance for another pal to come under the same brutal sway as he had? What sort of a friend was he, anyway? But an I.O.U.!... And in Lester Stark's name! He remembered the black looks that passed between the two of them that night, remembered them as though they had been but yesterday. He jerked his chin up.

"What're they going to do about it?"

"Headland told me to tell you that he was going to investigate the matter further. That you were to keep up your heart. ... Seemed a decent sort of a chap, I must say."

Keep up his heart!... And there was a chance of someone else taking his share of the damnable thing, after all!... But Lester Stark wouldn't *kill*. Perhaps not—and yet, some months ago he had told him to his face that he'd like to send Wynne's body to burn in hell!... H'm. Well, he would have to keep his mouth shut upon *that* conversation, at all events, or they'd have poor Stark by the heels the next minute. ... But somehow his heart had lightened. Cleek didn't seem such a bad chap, after all. And they couldn't hang him yet, anyhow.

For the rest of the long, dreary day the memory of that I.O.U. with Lester Stark's name sprawled across the bottom of it, in the dashing caligraphy that he knew, danced before his mind's eye like a fleeting hope, making the day less long.

CHAPTER XVIII
POSSIBLE EXCITEMENT

Meanwhile, Cleek, Mr. Narkom, and Dollops stayed on at the Towers for such time as it would take to have the coroner's inquest arranged, and Merriton brought up before the local magistrate.

Mr. Narkom was frankly uneasy over the whole affair.

"There's something fishy in it, Cleek," he kept saying. "I don't like the looks of it. Taking that innocent boy up for a murder which I feel certain he never committed. Of course, circumstantial evidence points strongly against him, but—"

"He's better out of the way, at all events," interposed Cleek. "Mind you, I don't say the chap is innocent. Men of Wynne's calibre have the knack of raising the very devil in a person who is under their influence for long. And there's Borkins's story." The queer little one-sided smile looped up his cheek for a moment and was gone again in a twinkling. He crossed to where Mr. Narkom stood, and put a hand on his arm. "Tell me," he said, quietly, "did you ever hear of a chap squirming and moaning and doing the rest of the things that the man said Wynne was doing in the garden pathway, when a bullet had got him clean through the brain? Something 'fishy' there, if you like."

"I should think so," replied Mr. Narkom. "Why, the chap would have died instantly. Then you think Borkins himself is guilty?"

"On the contrary, I do not," returned Cleek, emphatically. "If my theory's correct, Borkins is not the murderer of Dacre Wynne. Much more likely to be Nigel Merriton, for that matter. Then there's the question of this I.O.U. that I found on the body. Signed 'Lester Stark', and the doctor—Gad! what a loyal friend to have!—told me that Lester Stark, Merriton, and a little man called West were bosom friends and club-mates."

"Then perhaps the man Stark killed him, after all?" threw in Mr. Narkom at this juncture, and there was a tinge of eagerness in his excited tones, which made Cleek whirl round upon him and say, accusingly, "Old friend, Merriton has won your heart as he has won others'. You're dead nuts on the youngster, and I must say he does seem such a clean, honest, upstanding young fellow. But you're ready to convict any one of the murder of Dacre Wynne but Merriton himself. Own up now; you've a sneaking regard for the fellow!"

Mr. Narkom reddened.

"Well, if you want the truth of it—I have!" he said, finally, in an "I-don't-care-what-the-devil-you-think" sort of voice. "He's exactly the kind of chap I'd like for a son of my own, and—and—dash it! I don't like seeing him in the lock-up; and that's the long and short of it!"

"So long as it's only the long and short, and not the end of it, it doesn't greatly matter," returned Cleek. "Hello! Is that you, Dollops?"

"Yessir."

"Any news for me? Found that chap with the straggling black moustache that tried to do me in the other night? I've not a doubt that you've discovered the answer to the whole riddle, by the look upon your face."

Dollops cautiously approached, looking over his shoulder as though he expected any minute that the cadaverous face of Borkins would peer in at him, or that perhaps Dacre Wynne himself would rise from the dead and shake an accusing finger in his face. He reached Cleek and laid a timid hand upon the detective's arm. Then he bent his face close to Cleek's ear.

"Well, I've an inklin' that I'm well on to the untyin' of it, s'help me if I ain't!" he whispered in highly melodramatic tones.

Cleek laughed, but looked interested at once, while Mr. Narkom prepared to give his best attention to what the lad had to say.

"Traced the blighter wiv the straggling whiskers on 'is lip, anyway!" he said, triumphantly, casting still another glance over his shoulder in the direction of the door, and lowering his tones still further. "Caught a glimpse of 'im 'long by the Saltfleet Road this afternoon, Guv'nor, and thinks I to myself, 'You're the blinkin' blighter wot tried to do the Guv'nor in, are you? Well, you wait, my lad! There's a little taste of 'ell-sauce a-comin' your way wot'll make you sit up and bawl for yer muvver.' He'd got on sailorin' togs, Mr. Cleek, an' a black 'at pulled down low over one eye. Mate wiv 'im looked like a real bad 'un. Gold rings in 'is ears 'e'd got like a bloomin' lydy, an' a blue sweater, and sailor's breeches. Chin whiskers, too, wot were somethin like rotten seaweed. Oh, a 'eavenly specimen of a chap 'e were, I kin tell you!"

"On the Saltfleet Road, eh?" interposed Cleek, rapidly, as the boy paused a moment for breath. "So? My midnight friend is doubtless sailing for foreign parts, as the safest place when coroner's evidence begins to get too hot for him. And what then, Dollops?"

"Couldn't find out much else, Mr. Cleek, 'cept to trace the place where the beggar 'angs out, and that's a bit of a shanty just off Saltfleet Bay, an' a stone's throw from what looks ter me very like a boat-factory of some kind. Reckon the chap's employed there, as, from a casual chat wiv a sailorin' Johnny in the bar parlour of the 'Pig and Whistle', where I wuz a-linin' of me empty stummick (detectin' is that 'ungry work, sir!) wiv a sossage an' a pint o' four-and-er-'arf, this feller tells me that pretty near everyone around here works there. I arsked 'im wot they did, an' 'e says, 'Make boats an' fings, with now an' agin a little flurry in shippin' ter break the monotony.'.... Anyway, I traced the devil wot nearly got *you*, Guv'nor, and *that's* somefing. And if I don't give 'im a taste of the 'appy 'ereafter, well, my name's not Dollops."

Cleek laughed and laid a hand upon the lad's shoulder.

"You've done a lot toward unravelling the mystery, Dollops, my lad," he said. "A regular right-hand man you are, eh, Mr. Narkom? This evening we'll hie us to the Saltfleet Road and see what further the 'Pig and Whistle' can reveal to us. It'll be like the old times of the 'Twisted-Arm' days, boy, where every second held its own unknown and certain danger. Give us an appetite for our breakfast, eh?"

He laughed again, a happy, schoolboyish laugh which brought a positively shocked expression to Mr. Narkom's round face.

"My dear Cleek!" he expostulated. "Really, one might think that you actually enjoyed this sort of thing! One of these fine days, if you're not careful, you'll be caught napping, and it'll take all Dollops's and my ingenuity to get you out of the clutches. I do beg of you to be careful—for Ailsa's sake, if not for mine."

At mention of the name, for a second the whole look upon Cleek's face altered. Something came into his eyes that softened their keenness, something settled down over his countenance, wiping away the mirth and the grim lines together. He sighed.

"Heigho!" he said, softly, spinning round upon his heel and surveying Mr. Narkom with a half-smile upon his lips. "I will be careful, dear friend. I promise. And I have given my word to—her—as well. And that the life of Hamilton Cleek should be so precious to any such angel as that—well, it 'fair beats me', as Dollops would say. ... I'll be careful, all right. You may depend upon it. But Dollops and I are going to have a little outing on our own. We'll ransack the 'make-up' box after lunch and see what it can produce. And if we don't bring back something worth hearing to you on our return to-night, then I'll retire from Scotland Yard altogether and take a kindergarten class. ... Gad! I feel sorry for young Merriton. But there's no other course open to us at present but to keep him where he is. Coroner's inquest takes place to-morrow afternoon, and a lot may happen in the meantime."

Mr. Narkom gravely shook his head.

"Don't like the thing at all, Headland," he supplemented slowly, lighting a fresh cigarette from the stump of the other one, and blowing a cloud of smoke into the air. "There's something here that we haven't got at. Something *big*. I feel it."

"Well, you'll have that feeling further augmented before many more days are over, my friend," returned Cleek, meaningly. "What did the letter from Headquarters say? I noticed you got one this morning, and recognized it by the way the stamp was set on the envelope—though I must say your secretary is more than discreet. It looked for all the world like a love-letter, which no doubt your curious friend Borkins thought it was."

But if Cleek appeared in fine fettle at the prospect of a possible exciting evening with Dollops, Mr. Narkom's barometer did not register the same comforting high altitude. He did not smile.

"Oh, it had to do with these continual bank robberies," he replied with a sigh. "They're enough to wear a man right out. Seem so simple, and all that, and yet—never a trace left. Fellowes reports that another one took place, at Ealing. As usual, only gold stolen. Not a bank-note touched. They'll be holding us up in the main road, like Dick Turpin, if the robbers are allowed to continue on their way like this. It's damnable, to say the least! The beggars seem to get off scot-free every time. If this case here wasn't so difficult and important, I'd be off up to London to have a look into things again. Frankly, it worries me."

Cleek lifted a restraining hand.

"Don't let it do anything so foolish as that to you, old man," he interposed. "Give 'em rope to hang themselves, lots of rope. This is just the opportunity they want. Give orders for nothing to be done. Let 'em have a good run for their money, and by-and-by you'll have 'em so they'll eat out of your hand. There's nothing like patience in this sort of a job. They're bound to get careless soon, and then will be your chance."

"I wish I could feel as confident about it as you do," returned Mr. Narkom, with a shake of the head. "But you've solved so many unsolvable riddles in your time, man, so I suppose I'll just have to trust your judgment, and let your opinion cheer me up. Still. ... Ah, Borkins! lunch ready? I must say I don't like eating the food of a man I've just placed in prison, but I suppose one must eat. And there are a few very necessary enquiries to be gone into before the coroner's inquest to-morrow. The men have been up from the local morgue, haven't they?"

Borkins, who had tapped discreetly upon the door and then put in a sleek head to announce lunch, came a little farther into the room and replied in the affirmative. Save for a slight light of triumph which seemed to flicker in his close-set eyes, and play occasionally about his narrow lips, there was nothing to show in his demeanour that such an extremely large pebble as his master's conviction for murder had caused the ripples to break on the smooth surface of his life's tenor.

Cleek blew a cloud of smoke into the air and swung one leg across the other with a sort of devil-may-care air that was part of his Headland make-up in this piece.

"Well," said he, off-handedly, "all I can say is, I wouldn't like to be in your master's shoes, Borkins. He's guilty—not a doubt of it; and he'll certainly be called to justice."

"You think so?" An undercurrent of eagerness ran in Borkins's tone.

"Most assuredly I do. Not a chance for him—poor beggar. He'll possibly swing for it, too! Pleasant conjecture before lunch, I must say. And we'll have it all cold if we don't look sharp about it, Lake, old chap. Come along."

... They spent the afternoon in discussing the case bit by bit, probing into it, tearing it to ribbons, analysing, comparing, rehearsing once more the scene of that fateful night when Dacre Wynne had crossed the Fens, and, according to everyone's but Borkins's evidence, had never returned. By evening Mr. Narkom, note-book in hand, was suffering with writer's cramp, and complained of a headache.

As Cleek rose from this private investigation and stretched his hands over his head, he gave a sudden little laugh.

"Well, you'll be able to rest yourself as much as you like this evening, Mr. Lake," he said, lightly, trying the muscles of his right arm with his left hand, and nodding as he felt them ride up, smooth and firm as ivory, under his coat-sleeve. "I'm not in such bad fettle for an amateur, if anything in the nature of a scrap comes along, after all. Though I'm not anticipating any fighting, I can assure you. There's the morning's papers, and the local rag with various lurid—and inaccurate—accounts of the whole ghastly affair. Merriton seems to have a good many friends in these parts, and the local press is strong in his favour. But that's as far as it goes. At any rate, they'll keep you interested until we come home again. By the way, you might drop a hint to Borkins that I shall be writing some letters in my room to-night, and don't want to be disturbed, and that if he wants to go out, Dollops will post them for me and see to my wants; will you? I don't want him to 'suspicion' anything."

Mr. Narkom nodded. He snapped his note-book to, and bound the elastic round it, as Cleek crossed to the door and threw it open.

"I'll be going up to my room now, Lake," he said, in clear, high tones that carried down the empty hallway to whatever listener might be there to hear them. "I've some letters to write. One to my fiancée, you know, and naturally I don't want to be disturbed."

"All right," said Mr. Narkom, equally clearly. "So long."

Then the door closed sharply, and Cleek mounted the stairs to his room, whistling softly to himself meanwhile, just as Borkins rounded the corner of the dining-room door and acknowledged his friendly nod with one equally friendly.

A smile played about the corners of the man's mouth, and his eyes narrowed, as he watched Cleek disappear up the stairs.

"Faugh!" he said to the shadows. "So much for yer Lunnon policeman, eh? Writin' love-letters on a night like this! Young sap'ead!"

Then he swung upon his heel, and retraced his steps to the kitchen. Upstairs in the dark passageway, Cleek stood and laughed noiselessly, his shoulders shaking with the mirth that swayed him. Borkins's idea of a 'Lunnon policeman' had pleased him mightily.

CHAPTER XIX

WHAT TOOK PLACE AT "THE PIG AND WHISTLE"

It was a night without a moon. Great gray cloud-banks swamped the sky, and there was a heavy mist that blurred the outline of tree and fence and made the broad, flat stretches of the marshes into one impenetrable blot of inky darkness.

Two men, in ill-fitting corduroys and soiled blue jerseys, their swarthy necks girt about by vivid handkerchiefs, and their big-peaked caps pulled well down over their eyes, made their way along the narrow lane that led from Merriton Towers to Saltfleet Bay. At the junction with Saltfleet Road, two other figures slipped by them in the half-mist, and after peering at then from under the screen of dark caps, sang out a husky "Good-night, mates." They answered in unison, the bigger, broader one whistling as he swung along, his pace slackening a trifle so that the two newcomers might pass him and get on into the shadows ahead.

Once they had done so, he ceased his endless, ear-piercing whistle and turned to his companion, his hand reaching out suddenly and catching the sleeve nearest him.

"That was Borkins!" he said in a muttered undertone, as the two figures in front swung away into the shadows. "Did you see his face, lad?"

"I did," responded Dollops, with asperity. "And a fine specimen of a face it were, too! If I were born wiv that tacked on to me anatomy, I'd drown meself in the nearest pond afore I'd 'ave courage to survive it. ... Yus, it was Borkins all right, Guv'nor, and the other chap wiv him, the one wiv the black whiskers and the lanting jor—"

"Hush, boy! Not so loud!" Cleek's voice cut into the whispered undertone, a mere thread of sound, but a sound to be obeyed. "I recognized him, too," interrupted Cleek. "My friend of the midnight visit, and the plugged pillow. I'm not likely to forget that face in a day's march, I can promise you. And with Borkins! Well, that was to be expected, of course. The next thing to consider is—what the devil has a common sailor or factory-hand to do with a chap like Dacre Wynne? Or Merriton, for that matter. I never heard him say he'd any interest in factories of any kind, and I dare swear he hasn't. And yet, what's this dark stranger—as the fortune-tellers say—doing, poking his nose into the affair, and trying to murder me, just because I happen to be down here to investigate the question of the Frozen Flames?... Bit of a problem, eh, Dollops? Frozen Flames, Country Squires, Dark Strangers who are sailormen, and a butler who has been years in the family service; there you have the ingredients for quite a nice little mix-up. Now, I wonder where those two are bound for?"

"'Pig and Whistle'," conjectured Dollops. "Leastways, tha's where old Black Whiskers is a-makin' for. Got friend Borkins in tow as well ternight, so things ought ter be gittin' interestin'. Gawd! sir, if you don't looka fair cut-throat I an't ever seen one.

"Makes me blood run cold jist ter squint at yer, it does! That there moustache 'ud git yer a fortin' on the stage, I swear. Mr. Narkom'd faint if 'e saw yer, an' I'm not so certing I wouldn't do a bunk meself, if I met yer in a dark lane, so to speak. 'Ow yer does the expression fair beats me."

Cleek laughed good-humouredly. The something theatrical in his make-up was gratified by the admiration of his audience. He linked his arm through the boy's.

"Birthright, Dollops, birthright!" he made answer, speaking in a leisurely tone. "Every man has one, you know. There is the birthright of princes—" he sighed. "Your birthright is a willing soul and an unwavering loyalty. Mine? A mere play of feature that can transform me from one man into another. A poor thing at best, Dollops, but. ... Hello! Lights ahead! What is it, my pocket guide-book?"

"'Pig and Whistle'," grunted Dollops in a husky voice, glad of an excuse to hide his pleasure at Cleek's appreciation of his character.

"H'm. That's good. The fun commences. Don't forget your part, boy. We're sailoring men back from a cruise to Jamaica and pretty near penniless. Lost our jobs, and looking for others. Told there was a factory somewhere in this part of the world that had to do with shipping, and have walked down from London. Took six days, mind; don't forget that. And a devilish long walk, too, I reckon! But that's by the way. Your name's Sam—Sam Robinson. Mine—Bill Jones. ... Our friends are ahead of us. Come along."

Whistling, they swung up to the brightly lit little public-house, set there upon the edge of the bay. Here and there over the unruffled surface of the waters to the left of them, a light pricked out, glowing against the gloom. Black against the mouth of the harbour, as though etched upon a smoky background, a steamer swayed uneasily with the swell of the water at her keel, her nose touching the pier-head, a chain of lights outlining her cumbersome hulk. Men's voices made the night noisy, and numerous feet scuttled to and fro over the cobbles of the dockyard to where a handful of fishing boats were drawn up, only their masts showing above the landing, with here and there a ghostly wraith of sail.

Cleek paused a moment, drinking in the scene with his love of beauty, and then assumed his rôle of the evening. And how well he could play any rôle he chose!

He cleared his throat, and addressed his companion in broad cockney.

"Gawd's truf, Sammie!" he said. "If this fair don't look like a bit of 'ome. Ain't spotted the briny for a dog's age. Let's 'ave a drink."

Someone turned at his raucous voice and looked back over the curve of a huge shoulder. Then he went to the doorway of the little pub, and raised a hand, with two fingers extended. Obviously it was some sort of sign, for in an instant the noise of voices dropped, and Cleek and Dollops slouched in and up to the crowded bar. Men made room for them on either side, as they pushed their way in, eyeing them at first with some suspicion, then, as they saw the familiar garments, calling out some hoarse jest or greeting in their own lingo, to which Cleek cheerfully responded.

A little to the right of them stood Borkins, his cap still pulled low over his eyes, and a shabby overcoat buttoned to the neck. Cleek glanced at him out of the tail of his eye, and then, at sight of his companion, his mouth tightened. He'd give something to measure *that* cur muscle for muscle, strength for strength! The sort to steal into a man's room at night and try to murder him! The detective planted an arm—brown and brawny and with a tattooed serpent winding its way round the strong wrist to the elbow (oh, wonderful make-up box!)—on the edge of the marble bar, and called loudly for a drink. His very voice was raw and husky with a tang of the sea in it. Dollops's nasal twang took up the story, while the barmaid—a red-headed, fat woman with a coarse, hard face, who was continually smiling—looked them up and down, and having taken stock of them set two pewter tankards of frothing ale before them, took the money from Cleek, bit it, and then with a nod dropped it into the till and came back for a chat.

"Strangers, ain't you?" she said, pleasantly, leaning on the bar and grinning at them.

"Yus." Cleek's voice was sharp, emphatic.

"Thought so. Sea-faring, I take it?"

"Yus," said Cleek again, and gulped down the rest of his ale, pushing the tankard toward her and nodding at it significantly.

She sniffed, and then laughed.

"Want another, eh? Ain't wastin' many words, are yer, matey? 'Oo's the little 'un?"

"Meaning me?" said Dollops, bridling. "None of yer blarney 'ere, miss! Me an' my mate's been on a walkin' tooer—come up from Lunnon, we 'ave."

"You never did!"

Admiration mingled with disbelief in the barmaid's voice. A little stir of interest went round the crowded, smoky room and someone called out:

"Lunnon, 'ave yer? Bin walkin' a bit, matey. Wot brought yer dahn 'ere? An' what're sailor men doin' in Lunnon, any'ow?"

"Wot most folks is doin' nowadays—lookin for a job!" replied Cleek, as he gulped down the second tankard and pushed it forward again to be replenished. "Come from Southampton, we 'ave. Got a parss up to Lunnon, 'cause a pal told us there'd be work at the factories. But there weren't no work. Gawd's truf! What're sailormen wantin' wi' clorth-makin' and 'ammering' tin-pots? Them's the only jobs we wuz offered in Lunnon. I don't give a curse for the plyce. … No, Sammy an' me we says to each other"—he took another drink and wiped his mouth with the back of his hand—"we says this ain't no plyce for us. We'd just come over frum Jamaica—"

"Go on! Travellin' in furrin parts was you!" this in admiration from the barmaid.

"—and we ain't seein' oursel's turning inter land-lubbers in no sich spot as that. Pal told us there was a 'arbour down 'ere abahts, wiv a factory wot a sailorman might git work at an' still 'old 'is self-respec'. So we walked 'ere."

"Wot energy!"

Black Whiskers—as Dollops had called him—broke in at this juncture, his thin mouth opening in a grin that showed two rows of blackened teeth.

Cleek twitched round sharply in his direction.

"Yus—wasn't it? An', funny enough, we've plenty more energy ter come!… But what the 'ell is this factory work 'ere, any'ow? An' any chawnce of a couple of men gittin' a bit er work to keep the blinkin' wolf from the door? Who'll tell us?"

A slight silence followed this, a silence in which man looked at man, and then back again at the ginger-headed lady behind the bar. She raised her eyebrows and nodded, and then went off into little giggles that shook her plump figure.

A big man at Cleek's left gave him the answer.

"Factory makes electric fittin's an' such-like, an' ships 'em abroad," he said, tersely. "Happen you don't unnerstan' the business? Happen the marster won't want you. Happen you'll 'ave ter move on, I'm a-thinkin'."

"Happen I won't!" retorted Cleek, with a loud guffaw.

"S'welp me, you chaps, ain't none uv you a-goin' ter lend a 'and to a mate wot's out uv a job? What's the blooming mystery? An' where's the bloomin' boss?"

"Better see 'im in the mawning," supplemented Black Whiskers, truculently. "He's busy now. Works all night sometimes, 'e does. But there's a vacancy or two, I know, for factory 'ands. Bin a bit of riotin' an' splittin' uv state secrets. But the fellers wot did it are gorn now"—he laughed a trifle grimly—"won't never come troublin' 'ere again. Pretty strict, marster is. But good work and good pay."

"And yer carnt arsk fer more, that's wot I ses!" threw in Dollops in his shrill voice.

Now Cleek, all this time, had been edging more and more in the direction of Borkins and his sinister companion who were standing a little apart, but nevertheless were interested spectators of all that went on.

Having at last obtained his object, he cast about for a subject of conversation and picked the barmaid whose rallies met with the approval of the entire company, and who was at that moment carrying on a spirited give-and-take conversation with the redoubtable Dollops.

"Bit of a sport, ain't she, guv'nor?" Cleek remarked to Borkins, with a jerk of his head in the woman's direction. The butler whirled round and fixed him with a stare of haughty indignation.

"Here, you keep your fingers off your betters!" he retorted angrily, for Cleek had dug a friendly elbow into his ribs.

"Oh, orl right! No offence meant! Thought perhaps *you* wuz the boss, by the look of yer. But doubtless you ain't nuffink ter do wiv the factory at all. Private gent, I take it."

"Then you take it wrong!" retorted Borkins, sharply. "And I *have* something ter do with the factory, if you wants ter know. Like ter show your good manners, I might be able to get you a job—an' one for the little 'un as well, though I don't care for Londoners as a rule. There's another of 'em up at the place where I lives. I'm 'ead butler to Sir Nigel Merriton of Merriton Towers, if you're anxious to know who *I* am." His chest swelled visibly. "In private I dabbles a little in—other things. And I've influence. You men can keep your mouths shut?"

"Dumb as a blinkin' dorg!" threw in Dollops, who was close by Cleek's side, and both men nodded vigorously.

"Well, then, I'll see what I can do. Mind you, I don't promise nothink. I'll think it hover. Better come to me to-morrow. Make it in the evening for there's a h'inquest up at the Towers. My master's been copped for murderin' his friend, and I'll 'ave to be about, then. Ow'll to-morrow evening suit?"

Cleek drew a long breath and put out his hand. Then, as if recalling the superior station of the man he addressed, withdrew it again and remarked: "You're a real gent, you are! Any one'd know you was wot they calls well-connected. Ter-morrow it is, then. We'll be 'ere and grateful for yer 'elp. … Wot's this abaht a murder? Fight was it? I'm 'appy at that sort of thing myself."

He squared up a moment and made a mock of boxing Dollops which seemed to please the audience.

"That's the stuff, that's the stuff, matey!" called out a raw-boned man who up to the present had remained silent. "You're the man for us, I ses! An' the little 'un, too."

"Reckon I can give you a taste of fightin' that'll please you," remarked Borkins in a low voice. "Yes, Mainer's right. You're the man for us. … Good-night, all. Time's up. I'm off."

"Good-night," chorused a score of voices, while the fat barmaid blew a kiss off the tips of her stubby fingers, and called out after him: "Come again soon, dearie."

Cleek looked at Dollops, and both realized the importance of getting back to the Towers before the arrival of Borkins, in case that worthy should think (as was far from unlikely) of spying on their movements, and checking up on Cleek's progress in letter writing. It was going to require some quick work.

"Well, Sammy, better be movin' back to our shelterin' roof an' all the comforts of 'ome," began Cleek almost at once, and gulping down the last of his fourth tankard and slouching over to the doorway. A chorus of voices stopped him.

"Where you sleepin'?"

"Under the 'aystack about 'arf a mile from 'ere," replied Cleek glibly and at a venture.

The barmaid's brows knitted into a frown.

"'Aystack?" she repeated. "There ain't no 'aystack along this road from 'ere to Fetchworth. Bit orf the track, ain't yer?"

Cleek retrieved himself at once.

"Ain't there? Well, wot if there ain't? The place wot I calls a 'aystack—an' wot Lunnoners calls a 'aystack too—is the nearest bit of shelter wot comes your way. Manner of speakin', that's all."

"Oh! Then I reckon you means the barn about a quarter of a mile up the road toward the village?" The barmaid smiled again.

"That's it. Good-night."

"Good night," chorused the hoarse voices.

The night outside was as black as a pocket.

"Better cut along by the fields, Dollops," whispered Cleek as they took to their heels up the rough road. "Got to pass him. This mist will help us. That was a near shave about the haystack. I nearly tripped us up there. Awful creature, that woman!"

"Looks like a jelly-fish come loose," threw in Dollops with a snort. "There's ole Borkins, sir, straight ahead. 'Ere—in through this gap in this edge and then across the field by the side of 'im. ... Weren't such a rough night after all, was it, sir?"

Cleek sighed. One might almost have thought that he regretted the fact.

"No, Dollops," he said, softly, "it was the calmest night of its kind I've ever experienced. But we've gleaned something from it. But what the devil has Borkins got to *do* with this factory? What ever it is he's in it right up to the neck, and we'll have to dig around him pretty carefully. You'll help me, Dollops, won't you? Can't do without you, you know."

"Orlways, sir—orlways," breathed Dollops, in a husky whisper.

"Where you goes, I'm a-hikin' along by yer side. You ain't ever going ter get rid of me."

"Good lad!" and they redoubled their pace.

CHAPTER XX
AT THE INQUEST

Thursday dawned in a blaze of sunshine, and after the bleak promise of the day before the sky was a clear, sapphire-blue.

"What a day! And what a mission to waste it on!" sighed Cleek next morning, as he finished breakfast and took a turn to the front door, smoking his cigarette. "Here's murder at the very door of this ill-fated place. And we've got to see the thing out!"

He spun upon his heel and went back again into the gloomy hall, as though the sight of the sunshine sickened him. His thoughts were with Merriton, shut away there in the village prison to await this day of reckoning, with, if the word should go against him, a still further day of reckoning ahead. A day when the cleverest brains of the law schools would be arrayed against him, and he would have to go through the awful tragedy of a trial in open court. What was a mere coroner's jury to that possibility?

Then too, perhaps in spite of evidence, they might let the boy off. There was a chance in that matter of the I.O.U., which he himself had found in the pocket of the dead man, and which was signed in the name of Lester Stark. Stark was due at the inquest to-day, to give his side of the affair. There was a possible loophole of escape. Would Nigel be able to get through it? That was the question.

The inquest was set for two o'clock. From eleven onward the great house began to fill with expectant and curious visitors. Reporters from local papers, and one or two who represented the London press, turned up, their press-cards as tickets of admittance. Petrie was stationed at the door to waylay casual strangers, but any who offered possible light upon the matter, eye-witnesses or otherwise, were allowed to enter. It was astonishing how many people there were who confessed to having "seen things" connected with the whole distressing affair. By one o'clock almost everyone was in place. At a quarter past, 'Toinette Brellier arrived, dressed in black and with a heavy veil shrouding her pallor. She was accompanied by her uncle.

Cleek met them in the hall. Upon sight of him 'Toinette ran up and caught him by the arm.

"You are Mr. Headland, are you not?" she stated rather than asked, her voice full of agitation, her whole figure trembling. "My name is Brellier, Antoinette Brellier. You have heard of me from Nigel, Mr. Headland. I am—engaged to be married to him. This is my uncle, with whom I live. Mr. Headland—Mr. Brellier."

She made the introduction in a distrait manner, and the two men bowed.

"I am pleased to meet you, sir," said Brellier, in his stilted English, "but I could wish it were under happier circumstances."

"And I," murmured Cleek, taking in the trim contour and the keen eyes of this man who was to have been Merriton's father-in-law—if things had turned out differently. He found he rather liked his looks.

"There is nothing—one can do?" Brellier's voice was politely anxious, and he spread out his hands in true French fashion then tugged at his closely clipped iron-gray beard.

"Anything that you know, Mr. Brellier, that would perhaps be of help, you can say—in the witness box. We are looking for people who know anything of the whole distressing tragedy. You can help that way, and that way alone. For myself," he shrugged his shoulders, "I don't for an instant believe Sir Nigel to be guilty. I can't, somehow. And yet—if you knew the evidence against him—!"

A sob came suddenly from 'Toinette, and Brellier gently led her away. It was a terrible ordeal for her, but she had insisted on coming—fearing, hoping that she might be of use to Nigel in the witness box. By the time they reached the great, crowded room, with its table set at the far end, its empty chairs, and the platform upon which the two bodies lay shrouded in their black coverings, she was crying, though plainly struggling for self possession.

Brellier found her a chair at the farther side of the room, and stood beside her, while near by Cleek saw the figure of Borkins, clad in ordinary clothes. He tipped one respectful finger as Brellier passed him, and greeted him with a half-smile, as one of whom he thoroughly approved.

Then there was a little murmur of expectancy, as the group about the doorway parted to admit the prisoner.

He came between two policemen, very pale, very haggard, greatly aged by the few days of his ordeal. There were lines about his mouth and eyes that were not good to see. He was thinner, older. Already the gray showed in the hair about his temples. He walked stiffly, looking neither to right nor left, his head up, his hands handcuffed before him; calm, dignified, a trifle grimly amused at the whole affair—though what this attitude cost him to keep up no one ever knew.

'Toinette uttered a cry at sight of him, and then shut her handkerchief against her mouth. His face quivered as he recognized her voice, then, looking across the crowded room, he saw her—and smiled. ...

The jury filed in one after the other, twelve stout, hardy specimens of the country tradesman, with a local doctor and a farmer or two sprinkled among the lump to leaven it. The coroner followed, having driven up in the latest thing in motor cars (for he was going to do the thing properly, as it was at the country's expense). Then the horrible proceedings began.

After the preliminaries, which followed the usual custom (for the coroner seemed singularly devoid of originality) the bodies were uncovered, and a murmur of excited expectancy ran through the crowd. With morbid curiosity they pressed forward. The reporters started to scribble in their note-books, a little pale and perturbed, for all their experience of such affairs. One or two of the crowd gasped, and then shut their eyes. Brellier exclaimed aloud in French, and for a moment covered his face with his hands; but 'Toinette made no murmur. For she had not looked, *would* not look upon the grim terrors that lay there. There was no need for *that*.

The coroner spoke, attacking the matter in a business-like fashion, and leaning down from his slightly elevated position upon the platform, pointed a finger at the singed and blackened puncture upon the temple of the thing that was once Dacre Wynne. He pointed also to the wound in the head of Collins.

"It is apparent to all present," he began in his flat voice, "that death has been caused in each case by a shot in the head. That the two men were killed similarly is something in the nature of a coincidence. The revolver that killed them was not the same in both cases. In that of Mr. Wynne we have a bullet wound of an extremely small calibre. We have, indeed, the actual bullet. We also have, so we think, the revolver that fired the shot. In the case of James Collins there has been no proof and no evidence of any one whom we know being concerned. Therefore we will take the case of the man Dacre Wynne first. He was killed by a revolver-shot in the temple, and death was—or should have been—instantaneous. We will call the prisoner to speak first."

He lifted a revolver from the table and held it in the hollow of his big palm.

"This revolver is yours?" he said, peering up under his shaggy eyebrows into Merriton's face.

"It is."

"Very good. There has been, as you see, one shot fired from it. Of the six chambers one is empty." He reached down and picked up a small something and held it in the hollow of the other hand, balancing one against the other as he talked. "Sir Nigel, I ask you. This we recognize as a bullet which belongs to this same revolver, the revolver which you have recognized and claimed as your own. It is identical with those that are used in the cartridges of your revolver, is it not?"

Merriton bent his head. His eyes had a dumb, hurt look, but over the crowded room his voice sounded firm and steady.

"It is."

"Then I take it that, as this bullet was extracted from the head of the dead man, and as this revolver which you gave to the police yourself, and from which you say that you fired a shot that night, that you are guilty of his murder. Is it not so?"

"I am not guilty."

"H'm." For a moment there was silence. Over the room came the sound of scratching pencils and pens, the shuffle of someone's foot, a swift intake of the breath—no more. Then the coroner spoke again.

"Tell us, then," he said, "your version of what took place that night."

And Merriton told it, told it with a ring in his voice, his head high, and with eyes that flashed and shone with the cause he was pleading. Told it with fire and spirit; and even as the words fell from his lips, felt the sudden chill of disbelief that seemed to grip the room in its cold hand. Not a sound broke the recital. He had been given a fair hearing, at all events, though in that community of hard-headed, unimaginative men there was not one that believed him—save those few who already knew the story to be true.

The coroner stopped fitting his fingers together as the firm voice faltered and was finally silent, and shot a glance at Merriton from under his shaggy brows.

"And you expect us to believe that story, Sir Nigel; knowing what we do about the bad blood between you and the dead man, and having here the evidence of our own eyes in this revolver bullet?"

"I have told the truth. I can do no more."

"No man can," responded the coroner, gravely, "but it is that which I must admit I query. The story is so far-fetched, so utterly impossible for a rationally minded being—"

"But you must admit that he was not a rationally minded being that night!" broke in a quick voice from across the room, and everyone turned to look into Doctor Bartholomew's seamed, anxious face. "Under the influence of drink and that devil incarnate, Dacre Wynne, a man couldn't be answerable for—"

"Silence in the Court!" rapped out the coroner, and the good doctor was forced to obey.

Then the inquiry went on. The prisoner was told to stand down, amid a chorus of protesting voices, for, though the story was disbelieved, everyone who had come in contact with Merriton had formed an instant liking for him. No one wished to see him condemned as guilty—save those few who seemed determined to send him to the gallows.

Three or four possible witnesses were called, but nothing of any importance was gleaned from them; then Borkins was summoned to the table. As he pushed past 'Toinette's chair from the knot of villagers which surrounded him, his face was white, and his lips compressed. He took his stand in front of the jury and prepared to answer the questions which were put to him by the coroner. That man's method seemed to have changed since his questioning of Sir Nigel and he flung out his queries like a rapid-fire gun.

Borkins came through the ordeal fairly well, all things considered. He told his story of what he had said he had seen that night, in a comparatively steady voice, though he was of the type that is addicted to nervousness when appearing before people.

Cleek, at the back of the court, with Mr. Narkom on his right and Dollops on his left, waited for that one weak spot in the evidence, and saw with a smile how the coroner lit upon it. His opinion of that worthy went up considerably.

"You say you heard the man Wynne groaning and moaning on the garden pathway after he was shot, and then practically saw him die?"

"I did, sir."

"And yet, a man killed in that fashion, hit in that particular portion of the temple, always dies instantaneously. Isn't that rather strange?"

Borkins went red.

"I have nothing to say, sir. Simply what I heard."

"H'm. Well, certainly the evidence does dovetail in, and the doctors may have been wrong in this instance. We can look into that evidence later. Stand down."

Borkins stood down with something like a sigh of relief, and pushed his way back into his place, his friends nodding to him and congratulating him upon the way he had given his evidence.

Then Tony West was called, and told all that he had to tell of his knowledge of the night's happenings in a rather irritated manner, as though the whole thing bored him utterly, and he couldn't for the life of him make out why any one even dreamed that old Nigel had murdered a man. He told the coroner something of this before he finished, and as he returned to his place a murmur of approval went up. His manner had taken the public fancy, and they would have liked to hear more of him.

But there was another piece of evidence to be shown, and this took the form of a scrap of creased white paper.

It was waved aloft in the coroner's hand, so that everyone could see it.

"This," said the coroner, "is an I.O.U. found upon the dead man, for two thousand pounds, and signed with the name of Lester Stark. An important piece of evidence, this. Will Mr. Stark kindly come forward?"

There was a rustle at the back of the court, and Stark pushed his way to the front, his face rather red, his eyes a trifle shamefaced. As he came, Merriton was conscious of a quickening of his pulse, of a leap of his heart, though he loathed himself afterward for the sensation. His eyes went toward 'Toinette, and he saw that she was looking at him, with all the love that was in her soul laid bare for him—and all—to see. It cheered him, as she meant it should.

Then Stark took his place upon the witness stand.

"This I.O.U. belongs to you, I take it?" said the coroner, briskly.

"It does, sir."

"And it was made out two days before the prisoner met his death. The signature is yours?"

Stark bowed. His eyes sought Nigel's and rested upon the pale, lined face with every appearance of concern. Then he looked back at the coroner.

"Dacre Wynne lent me that money two days before he came down to visit Merriton. No one knew of it, except he and I. We had never been good friends—in fact, I believe he hated me. My mother had been—well, kind to him in the old days, and I suppose he hadn't forgotten it. Anyhow, there was family difficulty. My—my pater left some considerable debts which we found we were obliged to face. There was a woman—oh, I needn't go into these family things, in a place like this, need I?... Well, if I must—I must. But it's a loathsome job at best. ... There was a woman whom my father—kept. When he died he left her two thousand pounds in his will, and he hadn't two thousand pounds to leave when his debts were cleared up. We—we had to face things. Paid everything off, and all that, and then, at the last gasp, that woman came and claimed the money. The lawyer said she was within her rights, we'd have to fork out. And I couldn't lay my hands upon the amount just then, because it had taken pretty nearly all we had to clear the debts off."

"So you borrowed from Mr. Wynne?"

"Yes, I borrowed from Dacre Wynne. I'd sooner have cut my right hand off than have done it, but I knew Merriton was going to be married, and I wouldn't saddle him with my bills. Don't look at me like that, Nigel, old chap, you know I *couldn't*! Tony West has only enough for himself, and I didn't want to go to loan sharks. So the mater suggested Dacre Wynne. I went to him, in her name, and ate the dust. It was beastly—but he promised to stump up. And he did. I'm working now on a paper, to try and pay as much off as I can, and—a cousin is keeping the mater until I can look after her myself. We've taken a little place out Chelsea way. That's all."

"H'm. And you can show proof of this, if the jury requires it?" put in the coroner, at this juncture.

"I can—here and now." He thrust his hand into his pocket and drew out a sheaf of papers, tossing them in front of the coroner, who, after a glance at their contents, seemed to be satisfied that they gave the answer he sought.

"Thank you. ... And you have no revolver, Mr. Stark, even if you had reason for killing Mr. Wynne?"

Stark gave a little start of surprise.

"Reason for *killing* him? You're not trying to intimate that *I* killed him, are you? Of all the idiotic things! No, I have no revolver, Mr. Coroner. And I've nothing more to say."

"Then stand down," said the coroner, and Lester Stark threaded his way back to the chair he had occupied during the proceedings, rather red in the face, and with blazing eyes and tightly set lips.

A stream of other witnesses came and gave their stories. Brellier told of how he had been rung up by Merriton to ask if there were any news of Wynne's arrival at the house. Told, in fact, all that he admitted to know of the night's affair, and ended up his evidence with the remark that "nothing on earth or in heaven would make him believe that Sir Nigel Merriton was guilty of murder."

Things were narrowing down. There was a restlessness about the court; time was getting on and everything pointed one way. After some discussion with the jury, the foreman of it, a stout, pretentious fellow, rose to his feet and whispered a few hurried words to the coroner. That gentleman wiped his forehead with a silk handkerchief and looked about him. It had been a trying business altogether. He'd be glad of his supper. He got to his feet and turned to the crowded room.

"Gentlemen," he said, "in all this evidence that has been placed before us I find not one loophole of escape for the prisoner, not one opening by which there might be a chance of passing any other verdict than that which I am compelled to pass now; save only in the evidence of Borkins, who tells that the dead man groaned and moaned for a minute or two after being shot. This, I must say, leaves me in some doubt as to the absolute accuracy of his story, but the main facts tally with what evidence we have and point in one direction. There is only one revolver in question, and that revolver of a peculiar make and bore. I have shown you the instrument here, also the bullet which was extracted from the dead man's brain. Is there no other person who would wish to give evidence, before I am compelled to pronounce the prisoner 'Guilty'—and leave him to the hands of higher Courts of Justice? If there is, I beg of you to speak, and speak at once. Time is short, gentlemen."

His voice ceased, and for a moment over the room there was silence. You could have heard a pin drop. Then came the scraping of a chair, a swiftly-muttered, "I will! I will! I have something to say!" in a woman's voice shrill with emotion, and 'Toinette Brellier stood up, slim and tall in her black frock, and with the veil thrown back from her pale face. She held something in her hand, something which she waved aloft for all to see.

"I … I have something to say, Mr. Coroner," she said in a clear, high voice. "Something to show you, also. See!" She pushed her way through the crowd that opened to admit her, gaping at her as she came rapidly to the coroner's table and held out the object. It was a small-sized revolver, identical in every detail to that which lay upon the coroner's table. "That," she said clearly, her voice rising higher and higher, as she looked into Merriton's face for a single instant and smiled wanly, "that, Mr. Coroner, is a revolver identical with the one which you have there. It is the same make, the same bore—*everything*!"

"So it is!" For a moment the coroner lost his calm. He lifted an excited face to meet her eyes, "Where did you get it, Miss Brellier?"

"From the top drawer of the secrétaire in the little boudoir at Withersby Hall," she said calmly, "where it has always lain. You will find a shot missing. Everything the same, Mr. Coroner; *everything* the same!"

"It belongs to some member of your household, Miss Brellier?"

She took a step backward and drew a sharp breath. Then her eyes were fixed upon Merriton's face.

"It belongs to—*me*," she said.

CHAPTER XXI

QUESTIONS—AND ANSWERS

A murmur of amazement went round the room, like the sound of rising wind. The coroner held up his hand for silence.

"You say it is yours, Miss Brellier? This—this is really most remarkable—most remarkable! The revolver is of French make, is it not? You bought it abroad?"

"I did. Just before I first came to England. I had been travelling through Tunis before that, and—well, one doesn't like to be without these things. Sir Nigel's revolver came from India, I believe—through the agents of a French firm, the makers."

"But—" The coroner's voice was low-pitched, incredulous, "are you trying to tell us you fired a shot that night, Miss Brellier?"

She shook her head, smiling.

"No—that would be impossible. But my revolver has always lain in that little secrétaire, and I have never had cause to use it since I have been on this side of the Channel. I was in bed early that night, with a headache. My uncle will tell you that. He took me to my room and spent the rest of the evening in his study, as you have already heard from him. No, I cannot say I murdered Dacre Wynne. Though I would say that or anything to save Nigel. But I didn't discover that this little revolver of mine had ever been fired until yesterday, when I happened to go to my secrétaire for a letter which I had locked away in that particular drawer. Then I took it up and chanced to examine it—I don't know why. Perhaps because it was the same as Nigel's, I—" she choked suddenly, and bit at her lips for control. "Is there not a loophole *here*, sir, by which Sir Nigel might be saved? Surely it must be traced who used this revolver, who fired the shot from it?"

Her voice had risen to a piteous note that brought the tears to many eyes in that crowded room. The coroner coughed. Then he glanced enquiringly over at Brellier, who had risen from his seat.

"You have something to say about this, Mr. Brellier?"

Brellier made a clicking sound with his tongue.

"I'm afraid my niece has been wasting your time, sir," he said quietly, "because I happen to have used that little instrument myself five months ago. We had a dog who was hurt—you remember Franco,

'Toinette? And if you carry your mind back you will also recollect that he had eventually to be shot, and that I was forced to perform that unpleasant operation myself. He was dear to me, that dog; he was—how do you call it?—a true 'pal'. It hurt me to do this thing, but I did it. And with that revolver also. It was light. 'Toinette must have forgotten that I mentioned the matter to her.

"I am afraid this can have no bearing upon the case—though the dear God knows that I would do all I could to bring this terrible thing to an end, if it lay in my power. That's is all, I think."

He bowed, and sat down again, beckoning his niece back to her seat with a little frown. She cast a piteous look up into the coroner's face.

"I'm sorry," she said brokenly; "I had forgotten about that. Of course, it is true, as my uncle said. But I was so anxious—so anxious! And there seemed just a chance. You understand?"

"I do, Miss Brellier. And I am sorry that the evidence in this case is of no use to us. Constable, take the prisoner away to await higher justice. I must say that I think no other verdict upon the evidence brought forward could possibly be passed upon the prisoner than I have passed to-day. I'm sorry, Sir Nigel, but—one must do one's duty, you know. … We'll be getting back to the office, Mr. Murkford." He beckoned to his clerk, who rose instantly and followed him. "Good afternoon, gentlemen."

… And so the whole wearisome proceedings were at an end—and Cleek had spoken no word of that would-be assassin who had come upon him in the dark watches of the night and sought his life. He noted that Borkins looked at him in some surprise, but held his counsel. Borkins knew more than he had said upon his oath *this* day; of that Cleek was certain. Well, he would bide his time. There were other ways to work besides the open-handed fashion of the coroner's court and the policeman's uniform. He was due to meet Borkins that night and discuss the possibilities of being taken on to work at the electrical factory. Something might come out of that—something *must* come of that. It was impossible that the thing should be left as it was, and an innocent boy—he was certain of Merriton's innocence, in spite of the evidence against him—should be hanged.

As he stepped out into the growing twilight Cleek touched Mr. Narkom on the arm and then ran over to the van into which the prisoner was stepping, his guardians of the law upon either side of him, his face white, his shoulders bowed. 'Toinette stood a few steps distant, the tears chasing themselves down her face and the sobs drowning her broken words of comfort to him. He seemed barely to notice her, but at sight of Cleek he flung himself round, and gave a harsh laugh.

"And a damn lot of good *you've* done me, for all your fine reputation!" he said sneeringly, his face reddening. "God! that there should be such fools allowed to hold the law in their hands! You've made a mistake this time, Mr. Cl—"

"One moment!" Cleek held up a silencing hand as the name almost escaped Merriton's lips. "Officer, I'm from Scotland Yard. I'd like a word with the prisoner alone, if you don't mind, before you take him away. I'll answer for his safety, I promise. … Keep your heart up, boy; I've not done yet!" This in a low-pitched voice, as the two men dropped away from either side. "I've not done by a long shot. But evidence has been so confoundly against you. I'd hopes of that I.O.U., but the whole thing was so simply explained—and there were the proofs, you know. Still, there was no telling how the story would come out. But it was so obviously true. … Only, keep up your heart, lad; that's what I wanted to tell you. I'd swear on my oath you weren't guilty. And I'll prove it yet!"

Something like a sob broke in Merriton's voice. He held out an impetuous hand.

"I'm sorry, sir," he said jerkily, "but it's a devilish ordeal. What a life I've led this past week! If you only knew—could only realize! It tears a man's nerves to atoms. I've almost given up hope—"

Cleek took the hand and held it.

"Never do that, Merriton, never do that," he said softly. "I've been through the mill myself once—years ago now, but the scar still stays—and it'll be a bit more red hell for the present. But if there's any saving you, any proving this thing right up to the hilt, I'll do it. That's all I wanted to say. Good-bye, and—buck up. I'm going to speak to the little girl now, and cheer her up, too. You'll hear everything as it comes along."

He squeezed the hand, manacled so grimly to the other, and smiled a smile brimming over with hope and promise.

"God bless you, Mr.—Headland," Merriton replied, and as Cleek beckoned to the two policemen, took his stand between them and entered the closed vehicle. The door shut, the engine purred, and the car shot away up the road toward the local police-station, leaving the man and the girl staring after it, the same mute sorrow and sympathy shining in both pairs of eyes.

As it disappeared round a corner, 'Toinette turned to Cleek, her whole agonized heart in her eyes.

"Mr. Headland!" she broke out with a gush of tears. "Oh, m'sieur, if you did but know—could but understand all that my poor heart suffers for that innocent boy! It is breaking every minute, every hour. Is there nothing, nothing that can be done to save him? I'd stake my very life on his innocence!"

Cleek let his hand rest for a moment upon the fragile shoulder, and looked down into the pallid face.

"I know you would," he said softly, "for even I know and understand what the love of a good woman may do to a man. But, tell me. That story of the revolver—*your* revolver. You can vouch for it? Your uncle *did* kill the dog Franco with it? You can remember? Forgive me for asking, or questioning for a moment the evidence which Mr. Brellier has given, but I am anxious to save that boy from the hands of the law, and for that reason no stone must be left unturned, no secret kept silent. Carry your mind back to that time, and tell me if that is true."

She puckered her brows together as if in perplexity and tapped one slim, perfectly-manicured finger against her white teeth.

"Yes," she said at last; "yes, it was every bit of it true—every bit, Mr. Headland. For the moment, in that room of terror, I had forgotten poor Franco's death. But now—yes, I can remember it all fully. My uncle spoke the truth, Mr. Headland—I can promise you that."

Cleek sighed. Then:

"But it was *your* revolver he used, Miss Brellier? Try to remember. He said that he told you of it at the time. Can you recollect your uncle telling you that he used your revolver to shoot the dog with, or not? That is what I want to know."

She shrugged her shoulders and spread out her hands.

"It is so *difficile*. I am trying to remember, and the matter seemed then so trivial! But there is no reason to doubt my uncle, Mr. Headland, for he loves Nigel dearly, and if there was any way in which he could help to unravel this so terrible plot against him—Oh! I am *sure* he must have told me so, *sure*! There would be no point in his telling an untruth over that."

"And yet you can not recall the actual remark that your uncle made, Miss Brellier?"

"No. But I am sure, sure that what he said was true."

Cleek shrugged his shoulders.

"Then, of course, you must know best. Well, we must try and find some other loophole. I promised Merriton I'd speak a few words to you, Miss Brellier, just to tell you to keep up heart—though it's a difficult task. But everything that can be done, *will* be done. And—if you should happen to hear that I have thrown up the case, and gone back to London, don't be a bit surprised. There are other ways, other means of helping than the average person dreams of. Don't mention anything I have said to you to *anybody*. Keep you own counsel, please, and as a token of my regard for that I will give you my word that everything that *can* be done for Merriton will be. Good-bye."

He put out his hand and she laid her slim one in it. For a moment her eyes measured him, scanning his face as though to trace therein anything of treachery to the cause which she held so dear. Then her face broke into a wintry smile.

"I have a feeling, Mr. Headland," she said softly, "that you are going to be a good friend to us, Nigel and me. It is a woman's intuition that tells me, and it helps me to bear the too dreadful suspense under which we are all now labouring. You have my word of honour never to speak of this talk together, and to keep a guard on my tongue for the future, if it is to help Nigel. You will let me know how things go on, Mr. Headland?"

"That I cannot for the present tell. It will depend entirely upon how events shape themselves, Miss Brellier. You may hear soon—you may not hear at all. But I believe in his innocence as deeply as you do. Therefore you must be content that I shall do my best, *whatever* happens. Good-bye."

He gave her fingers a soft squeeze, held them a moment and then, dropping them, bowed and swung upon his heel to join Mr. Narkom, who was standing near by, the last of the group of interested spectators of that afternoon's ghastly business. Dollops stood a little back from them, awaiting his orders.

"We'll have some supper at the village 'pub,' my dear Lake," said Cleek in a loud, clear voice that carried to every corner of the deserted garden, "and then come back to the Towers long enough to pack up our traps and clear out of this haunted house altogether. The case is one too many for me, and I'm chucking it." Mr. Narkom opened his mouth to speak, but his colleague gave him no opportunity. "It's a bit too fishy for my liking," he went on, "when the only clues a man's got to go on are a dancing flame and a patch of charred grass—which, by the way, never struck me as particularly interesting at the best of times—and when evidence points so strongly toward young Merriton's guilt. All I can say is, let's go. That's the ticket for me."

"And for me also, old man!" agreed Mr. Narkom, emphatically, following Cleek's lead though rather in the dark. "It's back to London for me, whenever you're ready."

"And that'll be as soon as Dollops can pack my things and get 'em off to the station."

CHAPTER XXII

A NEW DEPARTURE

The question of packing was a very small matter altogether, and it was barely seven o'clock when, this finished, Cleek and Mr. Narkom had collected their coats and hats from the hat-stand, given Borkins the benefit of their very original ideas as to closing up the house and clearing out of it as soon as possible, each of them slipped a sovereign into his hand, and were standing talking a short while at the open front door. The chill of the evening crept into the house in cold breaths, turning the gloomy hall into a good representation of a family vault.

"All I can say," said Cleek, chewing a cigar, his hands in his trousers' pockets, and his feet rocking from toe to heel, "is—get out of it, Borkins, as soon as you can. I don't mind tellin' you, I'm jolly glad to be clearin' out myself. It's been a devilish uncanny business from first to last, and not much to my taste. Now, *I* like a decent robbery or a nice, quick-fingered forger that wants a bit of huntin' up. You know, even detectives have their particular favourites in the matter of crime, Borkins, and a beastly murder isn't exactly in *my* line."

Borkins laughed respectfully, rubbing his hands together.

"Nor mine, sir," he made answer. "Though I must say you gentlemen 'aven't been a bit what I imagined detectives to be. When you first come down, you know, I spotted something different about you, and—"

"Ought to be on the Force yourself!" supplemented Cleek.

"And not such a bad callin' neither!" returned Borkins with a grin. "But I knew you wasn't what you said you was, in a manner of speakin'. And if it 'adn't been for all this unpleasantness, it would 'ave bin a nice little change for yer, wouldn't it? Sorry to see the last of you, sirs, I am that. And that young gentleman of your'n. But I must say I'm glad to be done of the business."

Cleek blew a cloud of smoke into the air.

"Oh, you'll have another dose of it before you're entirely finished!" he responded. "When the case comes on in London. *That's* the ticklish part of the business. We'll meet there again, I expect, as Mr. Lake and I will be bound to give our evidence—which is a thankless task at the best of times. ... Hello! Dollops, got the golf-clubs and walking-sticks? That's a good lad. Now we'll be off to old London again—eh, Lake? Good-bye, Borkins. Best of luck."

"Good-bye, gentlemen."

The two men got into the taxi Dollops had procured for them, while that worthy hopped on to the seat beside the driver and gave him the order to "Nip it for the eight o'clock train for Lunnon, as farst as you kin slide it, cabby!" To which the chauffeur made some equally pointed remark, and they were off.

But Borkins either did not realize that the eight-o'clock train for London was a slow one, or thought that it was the most convenient for the two gentlemen most interested, because he did not give a thought to the matter that that particular train stopped at the next station, some three miles away from Fetchworth. And even if he had and could have seen the two tough-looking sailormen who descended from the first-class compartment there and stepped on to the tiny platform among one or two others, he would never have dreamed of associating them with the Mr. Headland and his man Dollops who had such a short time ago left the Towers for London.

Which is just as well, as it happened, for it was with Borkins that Cleek and Dollops were most concerned. Upon the probability of their friendship with the butler hung the chance of their getting work. They had left Mr. Narkom to go up to London and keep his eyes open for any clues in the bank robberies case, and had promised to report to him as soon as possible, if there were anything to be gleaned at the factory. Mr. Narkom had expressed his doubts about it, had told Cleek that he really did not see how any human agency could possibly get Nigel Merriton off, with such appalling evidence to damn him. And what an electrical factory could have to do with it ... !

"You forget the good Borkins's connection with the affair," returned Cleek, a trifle sharply, "and you forget another thing. And that is, that I have found the man who attempted my life, and mean eventually to come to grips with him. That is the only reason why I did not speak at the inquest this afternoon. I am going to bide my time, but I'll have the beggar in the end. If working for a time at an electrical factory is going to help on matters, then work there I'm going to, and Dollops with me. ...

"If there should be need of me, don't forget that I am Bill Jones, sailorman, once of Jamaica, now of the Factory, Saltfleet. And stick to the code. A wire will fetch me." He hopped out upon the platform just here, in his "cut-throat" make-up—a little hastily done, for the time between the stations had been short—but excellent, nevertheless; then as Mr. Narkom gripped his hand, he put his head into the carriage again.

"My love to Ailsa if you see her, and tell her all goes well with me, like a good friend!" whispered Cleek, softly.

Mr. Narkom nodded, waved his hand, and then the two navvies swung away from the train, gave up their tickets to the porter—having procured third-class as well as first for just this very arrangement—and after enquiring just how far it was to Saltfleet Bay, and learning that it was a matter of "two mile and a 'arf by road, and a couple o' mile by the fields," strode off through the little gate and on to the highroad. Just how adventurous their quest was going to turn out to be even they did not fully realize.

They reached the outskirts of the bay, just as a clock in the church tower half a mile away struck out nine, in deep-throated, sonorous tones.

To the right of them the "Pig and Whistle" flaunted its lights and its noise, its hilarious laughter and its coarse-thrown jests. Cleek sighed as he turned toward it.

"Now for it, boy," he said softly, and then started to whistle and to laugh alternately, making his way across the cobbles to the brightly-lit little pub. Someone ran to the doorway and peered out at sound of his voice, trying to penetrate the darkness and discover who the stranger might be thus gaily employed.

Cleek sang out a greeting.

"Good evenin' to yer, matey! This 'ers's Bill Jones and 'is pal. 'Ow, I'll tyke the 'ighroad, and you'll tyke the laow road! and I'll be in Scotland afore yer'. ... 'Ere, Sammie, me lad, come along o' me an' warm yer witals. I could drink the sea—strite I could!"

He heard the man in the doorway laugh, and then he beckoned to him to come along. And so they entered the "Pig and Whistle," and were greeted enthusiastically by the red-headed barmaid, while many voices went up to greet them, showing that already they had got on the right side of the men who were to be their fellow-workers.

"Gen'leman 'ere yet?" queried Cleek, jerking his thumb in the direction where Borkins had stood the night before. "I've what you calls an appointment wiv 'im, yer know. And. ... 'Ere the blighter is!

Good evenin', sir. Pleased ter see yer again, though lookin' a bit pale abaht the gills, if yer don't mind my sayin' so."

"And so would you be, if you'd been through the ordeal I 'ave this afternoon," snapped out Borkins in reply. "It's a beastly job a-tellin' people what yer seen and 'eard. It is indeed!"

"'Arder ter tell 'em wot you *'aven't* seen an' 'eard, all the syme, matey," threw in Cleek. "Done that meself, I 'as—bit of sleight-o'-'and what they'd pulled me up for out Whitechapel way when I was a kid. Seein' the master ternight, ain't we, sir?"

Borkins slopped down his tankard of beer and wiped his mouth before replying.

"Seen him already," he answered with a touch of asperity, "and told 'im about you both, I 'ave. 'E says you're ter go up to the foreman termorrow, say I sent you. Say the master 'as passed you, that'll be all right. Couple o' quid a week, and the chance of a rise if you're circumspect and keeps yer mouth closed."

"That's my gyme all right, guv'nor!" struck in Dollops shrilly, clapping his tankard down upon the bar with a loud bang. "Close as 'ouses we are, guv'nor. An' me mate's like a hoyster."

"Well, mind you remember it!" retorted Borkins sharply. "Or it'll go badly with the pair of you. That's fixed, then, ain't it? What's yer names again? I've forgotten."

"Bill Jones, an' 'im's Sammie Robinson," replied Cleek quickly. "I'm much obliged to yer, sir. Any one know where we kin get a shake-down for the night? Time enough ter look for lodgin's termorrer."

It was the barmaid's turn to speak, and she rested her rather heavy person against the bar and touched Cleek's shoulder.

"Mother, she 'as lodgers, dearie," she said in a coaxing voice. "You kin come along to us, and stay right along, if you're comfortable. Nice beds we 'ave, and a good 'ot dinner in the middle uv the day. You kin take yer breakfast with us. Better come along to 'er ternight."

"Thanks, I will," grunted Cleek in reply, and dug Dollops in the ribs, just to show him how pleased he was with the arrangement.

And so the evening passed. The lodgings were taken, the charge being moderate for the kind of living that men in their walk of life were used to, and the next morning found them both ensconced at their new work.

The overseer proved to be a big, burly man, who, having received the message from "the gentleman at the inn," immediately set them to work on the machinery. The task was simple; they had merely to feed the machine with so much raw material, and the other men and machines did the rest. But what pleased them more, they were put to work side by side. This gave Cleek a good opportunity of passing remarks now and then to Dollops and telling him to take note of things.

The factory was a smallish place, with not too large a payroll, and Cleek gleaned from that first morning's work that it was run solely for the purpose of making electrical fittings.

"Where do they ship 'em to, matey?" he asked his next-door neighbour, a pleasant-faced chap about twenty-three or four.

"Over ter Belgium. Big firm there what buys from the master."

"Oh?" So they were trading with Belgium, were they? That was interesting. "Well, then, 'ow the dickens do they send 'em out?"

"Boats, idiot!" The man's voice was full of contempt for the nincompoop who couldn't use his head. Above the clang of the machinery Cleek's voice rose a trifle higher.

"Well, any fellow would know *that*!" he said with a laugh. "But what I means is, what sort er boats? Big uns, I should sy, fer stuff like this."

The man looked about him and bent his head. His voice dropped a note or two.

"*Fishin'* boats," he said softly, and could be made to say no more, in spite of the scornful laugh with which Cleek greeted this news.

Fishing boats?… H'm. That was devilish peculiar. Sending out electrical fittings to Belgium in *fishing boats*! Funny sort of a way to do trade, though no doubt it was quite permissible up to a point. Well, he must glean something more out of this good fellow before the day was over.

A glass of beer at the "Pig and Whistle" after dinner worked wonders with the man's tongue. He was not a favourite, so free drinks did not often come his way. After the second glass he seemed almost ready to sell his soul to this amicable newcomer, but Cleek was wise, and bided his time. He didn't mean to fleece his man of the information in sight and sound of his fellows. So he simply talked of the topics of the day, discussed the labour question—from a new viewpoint—and then, as they strolled back together to the factory, just as the whistle began to blow that told the hands the dinner-hour was over, Cleek fired his first shot.

"See 'ere, matey," he began confidentially, "you're a decent sort of bloke, you are! Tell us a bit more about them there fishin' boats wot you spoke uv. I'm that interested, I've been fair eaten up with curiosity. Yer didn't mean the master of this plyce goes and ships electrical fittin's and such-like out to Belgium in *fishin'* boats—strite, eh?"

"Yus." Jenkins nodded. "That's exactly what I do mean. Seems sort er funny, don't it? And I reckon there's somethin' a bit fishy about the whole thing. But I keep me mouth shut. That overseer's the very devil 'imself. Happen you'll larn ter do likewise. Two chaps who were 'ere larst thought they'd be a bit smarty like, and told 'im they were goin' ter tell all they knew—though God knows what it was! I ain't been able to learn much, and haven't tried neither. But they went—zip! like that! Never saw 'em no more, and nothin' come of it. … Best to keep your mouth shut, mate. In this 'ere place, any'ow."

"Oh," said Cleek off-handedly, "I'm not one to blab. You needn't be afraid o' that. By the way, who's the chap with the black mustache a-stragglin' all over 'is fyce? An' the narsty eye? Saw 'im with Borkins, the man wot engaged me night before last."

"That wasn't Borkins, me beauty," returned Jenkins with a laugh. "That ain't his name. 'Ow did you come ter think of it? That fellow's name's Piggott. And the other man? We calls 'im Dirty Jim, because 'e does all the dirty work for the boss; but 'is real name's Dobbs. And if you takes my word for anything, pal, you won't go rubbin' 'im up the wrong way. 'E's a fair devil!"

H'm! "Dirty Jim," otherwise Jim Dobbs. And he was in the employment of this very extraordinary firm for the purpose of doing its "dirty work." Well, there seemed a good deal of employment for him, if that was the case. And Borkins was *not* Borkins in this part of the world.

Cleek stepped back to his work a little thoughtful, a little absent-minded, until the frown upon his forehead caused Dollops to lean over and whisper anxiously, "Nothin' the matter, is there, sir?"

He shook his head rapidly.

"No, boy, no. Simply thinking, and smelling a rat somewhere."

"Been smellin' of it meself this parst two hours," returned Dollops in a sibilant whisper. His eye shone for a moment with the light of battle. "Got summink ter tell you," he whispered under cover of the noise. "Summink wot ought ter interest yer, I don't fink. 'Ave ter keep till evenin'. Eh, Bill?"

"Right you are, matey." Cleek's voice rose loudly as the overseer passed, pausing a moment to watch them at work. "Nice job this, I must sy. Arfter me own 'eart, strite it is. Soon catch on to it, don't yer?"

"*Ra-ther!*" returned Dollops significantly.

The overseer, with a shrug of the shoulders, moved on.

CHAPTER XXIII
PRISONERS

It was not until the evening was fairly far advanced that the opportunity of speaking to Dollops alone was afforded Cleek. He took it when the "Pig and Whistle" was filled to overflowing, and hardly a man who worked at the factory was not inside it or standing outside near the little quay, holding the usual evening's confab on the affairs of the day. Cleek caught hold of Dollops as he was making his way into the little bar.

"Come fer a turn up the road, matey," he said loudly. "It's a fine evenin' wot mykes yer 'omesick fer a sight uf yer own fireside. 'Ave another drink later, mebbe. Come on."

Dollops linked arms with him, and, smoking and talking, the two men went off up the dark lane which led from the quayside, and of a night-time was as black as a pocket. Cleek's torch showed them the pathway, and as they walked they talked in rapid whispers.

"Now, lad, let's hear all you've got to say!" he rapped out at length, as the distance grew between themselves and the crowded little pub, and they were safely out of earshot.

Dollops gulped with pent-up excitement.

"Lor! sir, there's summink wrong, any'ow; I've discovered that much!" he broke out enthusiastically. "Chummed up with ole Black Whiskers I did, and promised 'im a 'and ternight at twelve o'clock ter do some loadin' on ter the fishin' boats wot's on their way ter Belgium. 'You're a nice-seemin' sort er lad,' he tole me after we'd bin chattin' fer ten minutes or so. 'Want ter make a bit of extra money by 'oldin' of your tongue?' I was on it like a knife. 'Ra-*ther!*' I ses. 'Orl right,' ses 'e. 'Come along ter the quayside ternight at twelve o'clock. There's a bit uf loadin' up ter be done, an' only a few uv the men are required. I don't choose none wot I don't cotton to.' 'You'll cotton ter me all right, matey,' I ses, with a sort uv a larf that seemed ter tickle 'im. 'I'm as close as the devil 'imself. Anythink yer doesn't want me ter see, just tip me the wink.' 'I will that,' ses 'e, and then went off. An' so 'ere I am, sir, fixed up for a busy evenin' along uv ole Black Whiskers. An' if I don't learn summink this night, well, my name ain't Dollops!"

"Good lad!" said Cleek, giving the boy's arm a squeeze. "That's the way to do it! And is that all you've got to tell me? I've done a bit myself, and chummed up with a chap called Jenkins, the tall, thin man who works on the left of me, and he's let me into the secret of the fishing boat business. But he's a close-mouthed devil. Either doesn't know anything, or won't tell. I'm not quite sure which. But he wasted a good deal of valuable breath endeavouring to teach me to keep my mouth shut. Gad! I'd give something to have a few moments alone with your friend Black Whiskers! There's a ripped pillow-case in my portmanteau which ought to interest him. And what else did you learn, Dollops?"

"Only that what they ships is electric tubin's ter perfect flexible electric wirin's wot is used for installations, sir," returned Dollops. "That's what most of the things were wot I set eyes on after workin'-hours, stacked up all ready ter be loaded on ter the boats. Long, thin things they were, an' ought ter be easy work, judgin' from their contents. But why they make all this mystery about it fair beats *me*!"

"And me into the bargain, Dollops," interposed Cleek, with a little sigh. "But there's an old saying, that there's no smoke without fire, and ordinary people don't make such a devilish fuss about others knowing their business if they're on the straight. What all this has got to do with the 'Frozen Flame' business I must confess somewhat puzzles me to discover. But that it *has* something to do with it is proved by that fishy character Borkins, and the amiable attempt of his friend to murder so humble a person as myself. Now it's up to me to find the missing link in the chain. ... Hello! here's a gap in the hedge here. Looks like it had been made on purpose. Let's go and investigate."

He whipped his little torch round and the circle of light flashing over the ground, revealed to their searching eyes something vastly unexpected in such a place and yet which, after all, seemed to fit into a place where so much mystery and secretiveness was in the air. They themselves, disguised as such rough characters, fitted into the strange picture, which struck Cleek, even in spite of his many peculiar cases, as very much out of the ordinary.

A gap in the hedge there was, right enough. And through the gap—someone must have been working here a very short time before—a square of turf, cut carefully out and laid upon one side, revealed to their astonished eyes a wooden trap-door, exactly suggestive of the pirates' den of a child's imagination, and with a huge iron ring fastened to the centre of it.

Cleek whistled inaudibly, and turning round upon Dollops a happy light in his eyes and a smile, almost of amusement on his lips.

"Gad!" he exclaimed softly. "Game to try this, Dollops. I am going to have a shot at it myself."

"But you ain't got no firearms on yer, sir, in case o' h'accidents," returned the literal minded Dollops, "and no man in 'is senses would attempt to go down that thing without 'em."

"Well, I've been called a lunatic before this, lad. And going down it I am, this minute. And if you've the least qualms at following me, you can just watch up here and warn me with the old signal if you hear any one coming. But I'm going down, to find out where this thing leads to, and a dollar to a ducat it'll lead to a good deal that means the unravelling of a riddle. The fellow who tangled the threads in the first place has a head any one might admire. But what I want to know is what he's taking all this trouble for. Coming, Dollops?"

Dollops sent a reproachful look into Cleek's face and sniffed audibly.

"Of course I'm comin', guv'nor," he made answer. "D'yer think I'd be such a dirty blighter as ter let you go dahn there—p'raps ter your very death—alone? Not me, sir. Dollops is a-follerin' wherever you lead, and if you chooses 'ell itself, well, 'e's ready ter be roasted and fried in the devil's saucepan, so long as 'e keeps yer company."

Without waiting for the end of this gallant, if rather prolonged speech Cleek knelt down, set his two hands upon the iron ring and pulled for all he was worth. But the ease with which the door lifted came as something of a surprise. It came up silently, almost sending Cleek over backward, as indeed it would have done a man with less poise, but he easily recovered himself. He and Dollops cautiously approached the edge, and in the half-light which the moon shed upon it (they did not use Cleek's torch) saw that a flight of roughly-made clay steps led down into darkness below. They sat back upon their heels and listened. Not a sound.

"Coming?" whispered Cleek in a low, tense whisper.

"Yes sir." Dollops was beside him in an instant. Cleek took the first step carefully, and very slowly descended into the darkness, with Dollops close behind him. Down and down they went, and on reaching the bottom, found the place opened out into a sort of roughly-made tunnel, just as high as a man's head, which ran on straight into the darkness in front of them.

"Gawd! gives yer the fair creeps, don't it?" muttered Dollops as they stood in the gloom and tried to take their bearings. "What yer goin' ter do, sir?"

"Find out where it leads to—if there's time," whispered Cleek rapidly. "We've got to find out what these human moles are burrowing in the earth like this for. I'd give a good deal to know. Hear anything?"

"Not a blinkin' sound, sir."

"All right. We'll try the torch, and if any one turns up we'll have to run for it. Now." He touched the electric button, and a blob of light danced out upon the rough clay floor, revealing as it swung in Cleek's swift fingers the whole circumference of the place from ground to ceiling.

"Cleverly made," muttered that gentleman in an admiring whisper. "It reminds me of the old 'Twisted Arm' days, Dollops, and the tunnels that ran to the sewers. Remember?"

"I should just jolly well think I do, guv'nor! Them were days, if yer like it! Never knew next minute if yer were goin' ter see daylight again."

"And this little adventure of ours seems a fair imitation of them!" returned Cleek, with a noiseless laugh. "Let's move a bit farther on and get our bearings. Hello! here's a little sort of cupboard without a door. And … look at those sacks standing there against that other side in that little cut-out place, Dollops. Now I wonder what the devil *they* contain. Talk about the Catacombs! They aren't in it with this affair."

Dollops crept up noiselessly and laid a hand upon one of the great sacks that stood one upon the other in three double rows, and tried to feel the contents with his fingers. It gave an absolutely unyielding surface, as though it might be stuffed with concrete.

"'Ard as a ship's biscuit, sir," he ejaculated. "Now I wonder what the dickens? … "

His voice trailed off suddenly, and he stood a moment absolutely still, every nerve in his slim young body taut as wire, every muscle rigid. For along the passage—not so very far in front of them, from where it seemed to terminate—came the thud of men's feet upon the soft clayey ground. The torch went out in an instant. In another, Cleek had caught Dollops's arm and drawn him into the narrow aperture, where, with faces to the wall, they stood tense and rigid, listening while the steps came nearer and nearer. They waited in the darkness, as men in the *Bonnet Rouge* days must have waited for the stroke of Madame Guillotine.

… The footsteps came forward leisurely. The intruders could hear the sound of muffled voices. One, brief, concise, clipping its words short, and with a note of cool authority in the low tones; the other— Dollops huddled his shoulders closer and contrived to whisper "Black Whiskers" before the two men came abreast of them. Strange to be walking thus comfortably in the dark! Either they were sure of their way that it didn't matter about having a light, or else they were afraid to use a torch.

"You will see that it is done, Dobbs, and done properly to-night?" sounded the brisk tones of "Black Whiskers'" companion. And then the reply: "Yes, it'll be done all right. We're sending 'em off at one o'clock sharp. Loadin' at twelve. No need to worry about that, sir."

"And these two newcomers? You can vouch for their reliability to keep their mouths shut, Dobbs? We wouldn't have chanced taking them on if we hadn't been so short-handed, but … you're sure of them, eh?"

They could hear "Dirty Jim's" ugly little chuckle. It seemed laden with sinister purpose.

"They're sound enough, master, I promise yer!" he made reply. "Ugliest-lookin' pair er cut-throats yer ever laid yer peepers on. Seen dirtier business than this, I dare swear. And Piggott's on to the right kind, all right. Good man, Piggott."

The two came opposite them, and stopped a moment, as though they might be wishing to investigate the contents of the sacks that stood nearby, hidden by the enveloping darkness. The tension under which Cleek and the youthful Dollops laboured was tremendous. Not daring to breathe they stood there hugging the wall, their every muscle aching with the strain, and then the two strangers walked on again, still talking in low, casual voices, until they had reached the end of the passage where the steps started abruptly upward. Then a patch of light showed suddenly.

"Steps here; be careful. They're none too easy," came the cautious voice of Black Whiskers. "I'll go up first, so's you kin follow in my steps. What's this? The door been left open, eh? I'll 'ave a few words with that chap Jenkins afore I'm many days older. I'll larn 'im to disobey 'is orders! Any one might come along 'ere and drop in casual-like!… The unreliable swine!"

The light grew less and less as the bearer of it climbed the rude stairs, and finally vanished altogether. And as it disappeared Dollops clutched Cleek's arm, his breath coming in little gasps.

"The door, sir—" he gasped. "If they close that, we're—" And even as he spoke there came a sound of sliding bolts and a thump which told the truth only too well.

"Did you 'ear, sir?" he almost moaned.

The trap door had been closed.

CHAPTER XXIV

IN THE DARK

Better men than they might have quailed in such a predicament. Here they were, at ten o'clock at night, shut in an underground passage that led heaven only knew where, and with, to say the least of it, small chance of escape. They might stay there all night, but the morning would probably bring release and—discovery. It was a combination which brought to them very mixed emotions.

Black Whiskers, should he be their rescuer might at once assume an entirely different rôle—would most likely do so, in fact. There was a grim element in this game of chance which they would just as soon had been absent.

Well, here they were, and the next thing would be to try their hands at escape on their own account. Perhaps the trap-door hadn't been tightly fastened down. It was a chance, of course.

"We'll try the trap-door end first, lad," said Cleek. "If that doesn't work we'll have a go at the other, but somehow you must get to the docks by midnight. You may learn the whole secret there, and it would be the worst luck in the world if you missed the chance; you mustn't. Come on."

"I seconds that motion," threw in Dollops, though in a somewhat forlorn voice. "I kin just imagine what it must be like to be a ghost tied up in a fambly vault, an' it fills me with a feelin' of sympathy for them creeturs wot I never felt before. Like a blooming messlinoleum this is!"

"Mausoleum, you grammatical wonder!" responded Cleek, and even in his anxiety he could not refrain from a laugh.

"Well, mausoleum or muskiloleum makes no difference to me, sir. What I wants ter know is—'ow do we get out of this charmin' little country seat? Try the trap-door, you ses. Right you are!"

He was up the rough steps like a shot, forgetful of the fact that, though the door might be closed, there might also be others strolling along in that secluded spot. Cleek came up now, behind him, and with a caution of silence steadied himself upon the step below, and pressed his shoulder up against the heavy door. He pushed and shoved with all his might, while Dollops aided with every ounce of strength in his young body.

The door responded not one whit. Black Whiskers had done his work well and thoroughly, possibly as an object-lesson to the absent Jenkins. And Jenkins, by the way, was the name of Cleek's new-found friend of the factory. H'm. That was cause for thought. Then Jenkins was more "in the know" than he had given him credit for. Possibly Black Whiskers knew already of their conversation at dinner-time. He'd have to close down on that source of information, at any rate—if they ever got out of this business alive.

These thoughts passed through Cleek's brain even while his shoulders and his strength were at work upon the unresponsive door. Only failure marked their efforts. At last, breathless and exhausted from the strain, Cleek descended the steps again. He listened, and, hearing nothing, signalled Dollops to follow him.

"They must have got in somewhere, and here's hoping it wasn't through this trap-door," he said evenly. "We'll see about it anyway. Unless they were as careful with the door at the other end. It's a sporting chance, Dollops my lad, and we've got to take it. I'll use my torch unless we hear anything. Then we'll have to trust to luck. Heaven alone knows how far this blessed affair runs on. We'll reach London soon, if we go on like this!"

"Yus, and find ourselves in Mr. Narkom's office, a-burrowin' under 'is 'Ighness' desk!" finished Dollops, with a little giggle of amusement. "And 'e wouldn't 'arf be astonished, would 'e, sir?… Crumbs! but the chaps wot made this bloomin' tube did their job fair, didn't they? It goes on forever. … Whew! I'm winded already."

"Then what you'll be by the end of this affair, goodness knows, my lad!" responded Cleek, over his shoulder. He was pressing on, hugging the wall, his eyes peering into the gloom ahead. "It seems to be continuing for some time. Hello! here's a turning, and the question is, shall we go straight on, or turn?"

"Seems as if them two blighters came round a turnin', judging from the nearness of their voices, sir," said Dollops, with entire sense.

Cleek nodded.

"You're right. … More sacks. If I wasn't so anxious to get out of this place so that you shouldn't be late for your 'appointment' with our friend Black Whiskers, I'd chance my luck and have a look what was in 'em. But there's no time now. We don't know how long this peculiar journey of ours is going to last."

They pressed on steadily along the rough, rudely made floor, on and on and on, the little torch showing always the few feet in front of them, to safeguard them against any pitfalls that might be laid for the unwary traveller. It seemed hours that they walked thus, and their wonder at the elaborateness of this extraordinary tunnel system grew. There were turnings every now and again, passageways branching off from the main one into other patches of unbroken gloom. And it was a ticklish job at best. At any moment someone might round the next corner and come upon them, and then—the game would be up with a vengeance. At Dollops's suggestion they followed always the turnings upon the right.

"Always keep to the right, sir, and you'll never go far wrong—that's what they teaches you in Lunnon. An' that's what I always follows. It's no use gittin' lost. So best make a set rule and foller it."

"Well, at any rate there's no harm in doing so," responded Cleek a little glumly. "We don't know the way out and we might as well try one plan as another. Seems pretty well closed up for the night, doesn't it? It certainly is a passage and if the door at the other end is impassable after all this wandering, I'll, I'll—I don't know."

"Carn't do no good by worritin', sir. Just 'ave to carry on—that's all we *kin* do," responded Dollops, with some effort at comfort. "There's summink in front of us now. Looks like the end of the blinkin' cage, don't it? Better investigate afore we 'it it too hard, sir."

"You're right, Dollops."

Cleek stepped cautiously forward into the gloom, lighting it up as he progressed, the rays of his tiny torch always some five feet ahead of him. And the end it proved to be, in every sense of the word. For here, leading upward as the other had done, was a similar little flight of clay-hewn steps, while at the top of them—Cleek gave a long sigh of relief—showed a square of indigo, a couple of stars and—escape at last.

"Thank God!" murmured Cleek, as they mounted the rough steps and came out into the open air, with the free sky above them and a fine wind blowing that soon dispelled the effects of their underground journey. "Gad! it's good to smell the fresh air again—eh, Dollops? Where on earth are we? I say—look over there, will you?"

Dollops looked; then gasped in wonder, astonishment, and considerable awe.

"The Flames, guv'nor—the blinkin' Frozen Flames!"

Cleek laughed.

"Yes. The Flames all right, Dollops. And nearer than we've seen 'em, too! We must be right in the middle of the Fens, from the appearance of those lights, so, all told, we've done a mile or more underground, which isn't so bad, my lad, when you come to look at the time." He brought out his watch and surveyed it in the moonlight. "H'm. Ten past eleven. You'll have to look sharp, boy, if you're to get to the docks by twelve. We've a good four miles' walk ahead of us, and—what was that?"

"That" was the sound of a man's feet coming swiftly toward them; they had one second to act, and flight over this marshy ground, filled with pit holes as it was, was impossible. No; the best plan was to stay where they were and chance it.

"Talk, boy—*talk*," whispered Cleek, and began a hasty conversation in a high-pitched, cockney voice, to which Dollops bravely made answer in the best tone he could muster under the circumstances.

Then a voice snapped out at them across the small distance that separated them from the unseen stranger, and they stiffened instinctively.

"What the hell are you doing here?" it called. "Don't you know that it's not safe to be in this district after nightfall? And if you don't—well, a pocketful of lead will perhaps convince you!"

From the darkness ahead of them a figure followed the voice. Cleek could dimly discern a tall, slouchy-shouldered man, clad in overalls, with a cap pulled down close over his eyes, and in the grasp of his right hand a very businesslike-looking revolver.

Cleek thought for a moment, then plunged bravely in.

"Come up from the passage, sir," he responded curtly. "Loadin' up ternight, and some fool locked t'other end before me and my mate 'ere 'ad finished our work. 'ad to come along this w'y, or else spend the rest of the night dahn there, and we're due for loadin' the stuff at the docks at midnight. Master'll be devilish mad if 'e finds us missin'."

It was a chance shot, but somehow chance often favours the brave. It told. The man lowered his revolver, gave them a quick glance from head to toe, and then swung upon his heel.

"Well, better clear out while there's no danger," he returned sharply. "Two other men are on the watch-out for strangers. Take that short cut there"—he pointed to the left—"and skirt round to the road. Quarter of a mile'll bring you. Chaps at your end ought to see to it that none of the special hands stray up this way. It's not safe. Good-night."

"Good-night," responded Cleek cheerily. "Thank you, sir;" and, taking Dollops's arm, swung off in the direction indicated, just as quick as his feet could carry him.

They walked in silence for a time, their feet making no sound in the marshy ground, when they were well out of earshot—Cleek spoke in a low tone.

"Narrow shave, Dollops!"

"It was that, sir. I could fair feel the razor aclippin' a bit off me chin, so ter speak. 'Avin' some nice adventures this night, ain't we, guv'nor?"

"We certainly are." Cleek's voice was absent-minded, for his thoughts were working, and already he was beginning to tie the broken threads of the skein that he had gathered into a rough cord, with here and there a gap that must—and should—be filled. It was strange enough, in all conscience. Here were these underground tunnels leading, "if you kept to the right," from a field out Saltfleet way, to the very heart of the Fens themselves. And what went on here in these uninhabited reaches of the marshland? Nothing that could be seen by daylight, for he had traversed every step of them, and gained no information for his pains. Therefore there could be no machinery, or anything of that sort. H'm. It was a bit of a facer, true; but of one thing he was certain. Somehow, in some way, the Frozen Flames played their part. That factory at Saltfleet and the fishing boats and the Fens were all linked up in one inexplicable chain, if one could only find the key that unlocked it. And what was a man doing out there at night, with a revolver? What business was he up to? And he had said there were two others on the look-out, as well.

Cleek pulled out a little blackened clay pipe, which was part of his make-up as Bill Jones, and, plugging it with tobacco, began to smoke steadily. Dollops, casting a sideways glance at his master, knew what this sign meant, and spoke never a word, until they had left the Fens far behind them and were well on their way toward the docks, and the "appointment" with Black Whiskers at twelve o'clock. Then:

"Notice anything, Dollops?" Cleek asked, slewing round and looking at the boy quizzically.

"How do you mean, sir?"

"Why, when you got to the top of those little steps and came out into the Fens."

"Only the Frozen Flames, sir. Why?"

"Oh, nothing. It'll keep. Just a little thing I saw that led me a long way upon the road I'm trying to travel. You'll hear about it later. Time's getting on, Dollops, my lad. You're due with your friend Black Whiskers in another ten minutes—and we're about that from the dockyard. Wonder if there'd be any chance of me lending a hand?"

Dollops thought a moment.

"You might try, sir—'twould do no 'arm, anyway," he said after a pause. "Pertickler as you're my mate, so ter speak. Ought ter be able to work it, I should think. … Look. Who's a-comin' now? If it ain't ole Black Whiskers 'imself!"

And Black Whiskers it was, to be sure. He lounged up to them, hands in pockets, hat pulled well down over his eyes, a sinister, ugly figure. He had an "air"—and it was by no means a pleasant one.

"Hullo, youngster!" he called out in a harsh voice. "Been seein' the country—eh? Better fer you and yer mate if yer keeps yer eyes well on the ground in this part uv the world. Never meddle in someone else's business. It don't pay." His voice lowered suddenly, and he jerked a thumb back over his shoulder. "Mate on the square with you, I s'pose? Comin' along now?"

"Bet yer life I am!" responded Dollops heartily, giving him a significant wink. "'Course I ain't said nuffin' ter ole Bill abaht what you tole me, but I know 'e's a cute un. No flies on ole Bill, guv'nor, give yer me oath on that. What abaht it, now? Shall us bring him along too? Just as you ses, guv'nor, seein' as you're the boss, but 'e's a strong fellow is my mate—and 'is mouth's like a trap."

Black Whiskers switched round in his slouchy walk, where he had fallen in step beside Dollops, leaving Cleek on the boy's right hand, and gave the "mate" a searching look under black brows. In the darkness, with just a thread of moonlight to make patterns upon the black waters and etch out the outline of mast and funnel and hull against the indigo, Cleek recognized that look, and set his mouth grimly. He'd seen it once before, upon that night when this man had stolen into his room and tried to knife him.

"Where're you off to, matey? With all your fine secrets? I'd like to know!" he said jokingly, digging Dollops in the ribs, and giving a loud guffaw. "Some girl, I suppose."

"Somethin' uv more account than women, I kin tell ye!" threw in

Black Whiskers roughly. "'E's going ter help me with a little work— overtime is what 'e'll get fer it. If yer willin' ter lend a 'and, over-time you'll get, too. But you'll keep yer mouth shut, or clear. One or t'other. It's up ter you ter choose."

Cleek laughed.

"Call me a fool, matey—but not a damned fool!" he said pleas-antly. "Bill Jones knows what side 'is bread's buttered on, I kin tell yer! Soft job like this one wot we've nicked on ter ain't goin' ter slip through 'is fingers fer a little tongue-waggin'. I'm on, mate."

"Righto."

"What's the job?"

"Loadin' up boats fer cargo."

"Oh!… Contraband, eh, matey?"

"That's none uv yer business, my man, and as long as you remem-bers that, you'll 'old yer job; no more, no less."

"Beg pardon, I'm sure. But I bin in the same sort uv thing meself— out in Jamaica. Used ter smuggle things through the customs. Nifty business it were, too, and I almost got caught twice. But I slipped it somehow. Just loadin' is our game, then?"

"*Jist loadin'*," responded Black Whiskers significantly. "'Ere we are. Now then, get ter work. See them tubings over there? Well, they've got to be carried over to that fishin'-smack drawn up against the dock. There's six of 'em goin' ternight, and we've got ter be quick. Ain't as easy as it looks, mate, but—that's not your business neither. Get ter work!"

They got to work forthwith, and turned to the pile of electrical tubings which was built up against the side of the dock wall, twice as high as a man's head. A pale lantern swung from the edge of the same wall, above them, hanging suspended from a nail; another hung on the opposite side from a post. By the light of these two lamps they could see a knot of men assembled in the centre of the dockyard, talking together in low whispers, while down below, at the water's edge, rocked a fleet of fishing boats awaiting their mysterious cargo. One could hear the men stirring restlessly and shifting sail as they waited for the task to begin.

Then the word was given in a low, vibrant voice, and they went to work.

"Easy job this, matey," whispered Dollops as he and Cleek advanced upon the stack of tubings and each started to lift one down.

"I ... Gawd's truf! *ain't* it 'eavy! Lorlumme! Now, what in blazes—?"

Cleek put up a warning finger, and shouldered the thing. Heavy it certainly was, though of such fine metal that its weight seemed incredible. And when one knew that these things carried electric wiring. ... Or *did they?*... Never was made an electric wire that was as heavy as that.

Cleek carried one of these tubings to the dock's edge, with the aid of Dollops handed it over into the hands that were outstretched to receive it, and went back for another one. Back and forth and back and forth they went, lifting, carrying, delivering, until one boat was loaded, and another one hove into sight in its place. He watched the first one's slow progress out across the murky waters for a moment, making a pretense of mopping his forehead with his handkerchief meanwhile. It was loaded *below* the water-mark! It hung so low in the water that it looked a mere smudge upon the face of it, a ribbon of sail flapping from its slender mast.

Electrical tubings, eh? Faugh! a pretty story that. ...

Two boats were filled, three, four. ... A fifth came riding up under the very nose of the last, and settled itself with a rattle of chains and bumping of sides against the quay. That, too, was loaded to its very edge, and took its way slowly out beneath their eyes. The sixth took its place after its fellows.

For a moment or two the sweating men ceased in their work, and stood wiping their faces or leaning against the dock wall, talking in low whispers.

Cleek and Dollops stood at the quayside, listening to the water lapping against the iron girders, and straining their eyes to catch a last glimpse of the fleet of fishing boats. Of a sudden from out the blackness others appeared. Old Black Whiskers gave a muttered order, and like a well-drilled army the men were ready again, this time flocking to the side of the quay as the boats rode up, and waiting for them, empty-handed. Cleek turned to the nearest one, and spoke in a low-toned voice.

"What now, matey? I'm new at this gyme."

"Oh—unloadin'. Usual thing. Faulty gauge. Don't never seem as though the factory kin get the proper gauge fer those tubin's. All the time I bin 'ere—nigh on to two years—it's bin the same. Every lot goes out, some comes back again with a complaint. Funny thing, ain't it?"

"Yus," responded Cleek shortly. "Damn funny." It certainly was. Unless … he sucked in his breath and his lips pursed themselves up to whistle. But no sound came.

And the work of unloading began.

CHAPTER XXV

THE WEB OF CIRCUMSTANCE

For a few days there was no more overtime to be earned by Cleek or Dollops, so that they were free to spend their evening as they wished, and though the "Pig and Whistle" got its fair share of their time—for the sake of appearances—there were long hours afterward, between the last tattered remnants of the night and the day's dawning, when they did a vast amount of exploration.

That they made good use of this time was proved by the little note-book that rested in Cleek's pocket, and in which a rough chart of the country and the docks was drawn—though there were still some blanks to be filled in—while opposite it was a rude outline of the secret passage into which they had blundered three nights before.

"Got to explore that hole from end to end, Dollops," said Cleek on the fourth evening, as they struck off together toward that gap in the hedge, soon after the clock in the village had chimed out ten, and the little bar of the "Pig and Whistle" was slowly emptying itself of its *habitués*. "I've the main route fairly correct, I think, and a rough idea of where those sacks stood, and where we took to cover when Black Whiskers was showing the master of this underworld domain through it. Happen to have learnt the chap's name yet?"

Dollops nodded.

"Yessir. Brent it is, Jonathan Brent, or so one of the men tells me. Says he's never seed 'im, though; nobody 'ardly ever does, from all accounts 'e give me. Ole Black Whiskers and our silent-footed friend Borkins is the main ones wot does 'is work for 'im."

"H'm. Well, that's something gleaned, anyway. Of course we may be able to find out who he really is, but the chances are small. Men like this chap don't go giving away anything more than they can help. They lie low and let their paid underlings stand the racket if it happens to come along. I know the type. I've come cross it before. Well, here we are. Now for it—but this time I happen to have brought along a revolver."

He crept through the hedge and crouching behind it ran to the spot where they had found the open trap-door upon that memorable occasion three nights before. There was nothing to be seen. The ground presented an absolutely unbroken appearance, so far as they could make out in the moon's rays.

"Clever devils!" snapped out Cleek, in angry tribute. "We'll have to use artificial light after all; but keep your torch light on the ground. It won't do for any one to spot us just now."

For perhaps a moment or two they explored the ground inch by inch, crawling round in the long grass upon their hands and knees, until a little tuft of brown earth sticking up through a piece of turf, like the upturned corner of a rug, showed them what they were looking for. With infinite care Cleek lifted up the square of turf and set it upon one side. The sight of the flat dark surface of the trap-door rewarded them. He ran his fingers along the two sides of it, and discovered a bolt, shot this, and then catching the iron ring once more in his hands, swung the top upward and laid it back upon the grass.

A minute more found them once more in the cavernous, breathless depths. Cleek handed the torch to Dollops.

"You hold that while I do a bit of sketching," he said, fidgeting in his coat-pocket for his fountain-pen. He then snapped open the flap of the note-book and began to sketch rapidly as they moved forward. Cleek was an adept in drawing to scale. The thing took shape as they continued their progress, keeping this time to the left instead of to the right. Cleek paced off the distance and stopped every now and then to check up results.

The place was as silent as the grave. Obviously no one was about here upon these nights when there was no loading and unloading going on. In that, at least, chance had been a good friend to them. They were going to make the most of it. Through little runways, narrower than the main route, and so low that they had to bend their necks to get along in safety, they went, measuring and examining. Every few yards or so they would come upon another little niche, stacked high with sacks of a similar hardness to those others back there at the beginning of their journey. Cleek prodded one with his finger, hesitated, then slipping out a penknife, slit a fragment of the coarse sacking and inserted his thumb. ...

He pulled it out with a look of astonishment upon his face.

"Hello, hello!" he exclaimed. "So that's it, is it? Gad! This is the approved hiding-place! Then those tubings—Dollops, just a little more of this wearisome search, just a few telephone calls to be made, and I believe I shall have untied at least *one* part of this strange riddle.

And when that knot is unfastened, it will surely lead me to the rest. … Go on, boy."

They went on, stepping carefully, and hesitating now and again to listen for any sound of alien footsteps. But the place might have been the grave for any sign of human habitation that there was. They had it to themselves that night, and made the most of it.

For some time they walked on, taking the road that most appealed to them, and in the maze must surely have retraced their own footsteps. Of a sudden, however, they broke into a sort of rough stone passage, with concrete floor that ran on for a few yards and ended at a flight of well-made stone steps, above which was a square of polished oak, worm-eaten, heavily-carved, and surely not of this generation's make or structure.

"Now, what the dickens … ?" began Cleek, and stopped.

Dollops surveyed it with his head on one side.

"Seems ter me, sir," he began, after a pause, "that this yere's the genuyne article. One of them old passages what people like King Charles and Bloody Mary an' a few other of them celebrities you sees at Madame Tussord's any day in the week, used to 'ide in when things were a-gettin' too 'ot fer 'em. That's what this is."

"Your history's a bit rocky, but your ideas are all right," returned Cleek with a little smile, as he stood looking up at the square of black oak above them. "I believe you're right, Dollops. It must have given the later arrivals a big start in that tunnelling business, or else they've been at it, or both. There must be years' work in this system of passageways. It is marvelous. But if it's a genuine old secret passage, those stairs will probably lead up into a house, and—let's try 'em. If the house they lead into is the one I think it is. … Well, we'll be unravelling the rest of this riddle before the night is out!"

So saying, he fairly leapt up the little flight of stone stairs, and then let his fingers glide over the smooth polished face of the oak door, pushing, probing, pressing it, a frown puckering his brows.

"If this *is* a genuine old secret hiding-place," he remarked, "then according to all the rules of the game there ought to be some sort of a spring *this* side to open it, so that the hidden man might be able to get out again when he wanted to. But where? Faugh! My fingers must be losing their cunning, and—Ah, here it is! Bit of wood gives way here, Dollops. Just a gentle pressure, and—here we are!"

And here they were, indeed, for as he spoke, the door slid back into the flooring out of sight, and they found themselves looking up into a room which was lighted by a single gas-jet, which barely illumined it, but which, when Cleek poked his head up above the flooring and took a casual survey of the place proved to be no less a place than the back kitchen of Merriton Towers!

He brought his head down again with a jerk, touched the spring in the edge of oak-panelling at the left of him, and let the door swing back across the opening once more; and not till it had slipped into place with a little *click* did he turn upon Dollops.

"*Merriton Towers!*" he ejaculated finally. "Merriton Towers! Now, if young Merriton really *is* a party to this thing that is going on down here in the bowels of the earth, why—Dash it, it's going to prove an even worse case against him than we knew! A chap who plays an underhanded game like this doesn't mind what he walks over to attain his ends. But ... Merriton Towers ... !"

He stopped speaking suddenly, sucked in his breath, his face turned very grim. Dollops broke the silence that fell, a tremour of excitement in his low-pitched voice.

"Yus—but it's the *back-kitchen*, sir," he threw out eagerly, like all the rest of them anxious if possible to shield the man who seemed to have won so many hearts. "And the back-kitchen don't spell Sir Nigel, sir. It's Borkins wot's at the bottom of *that*, and—"

"Maybe, maybe," interposed Cleek, a trifle hastily, but the grim look did not leave his face. "But if anything as curious as all this affair turns up in the evidence it won't help the boy any, that is a certainty. ... Merriton Towers!"

He swung upon his heel and quickly retraced his steps, until the little stone passageway was left behind them, and a few feet ahead loomed up another of those queer turnings, which led—who knew where?

"We'll take it on chance," said Cleek as they paused, while he marked it in his chart, "and follow our noses. But I confess I've had a shock. I never thought—never even dreamt of Merriton Towers being connected with this smuggling or, whatever it is, Dollops! And if I hadn't been down in that very kitchen upon a voyage of discovery the other day, I'd have had more reason to disbelieve the evidence of my own eyes. The light was on, too. Lucky for us we didn't pop our heads up at the moment when someone was there. But then the servants are all gone. Borkins is keeping the house open until after the trial. So it was Borkins who was using that light, that's pretty obvious; and our necks have been spared by an inch or two less than I had imagined. We must hurry; time's short, and there's a good deal to be got through this night, I can tell you!"

"Yessir," said Dollops, not knowing what else to say, for Cleek was keeping up a sort of running monologue of his ideas of the case. "Don't think much uv this 'ere passage, anyway, do you?"

"No—narrower than the rest. But it may end just where we want to go. 'Journeys end in lovers' meetings' the poet sings, but not this kind of a journey—no, not exactly. We'll find the hangman's rope at the end of this riddle, Dollops, or I'm very much mistaken; and I've an uncomfortable idea as to who will swing in the noose."

For some time after that they pressed on in silence. Here and there along the passage the walls opened out suddenly into little cut-out places filled as ever with their built-up sacks. Each time Cleek passed them he chuckled aloud, and then—once more his face would become grim. For some moments they groped along in the gloom, their heads bent, to prevent them bumping the low mud ceiling, their lips silent, but in the hearts of each a sort of dull dread. Merriton Towers! Borkins, perhaps. But what if Borkins and Merriton had been working hand-in-glove, and then, somehow or other, had had a split? That would account for a good deal, and in particular the man's attitude toward his master. … Cleek's brain ran on ahead of his feet, his brows drew themselves into a knot, his mouth was like a thin line of crimson in the granite-like mask of his face.

Of a sudden he stopped and pointed ahead of him. Still another flight of stairs met their eyes, but they were of newer, more recent make, and composed of common deal, unvarnished and mudstained with the marks of many feet up and down their surface.

Cleek drew a deep breath, and his face relaxed.

"The end of the journey, Dollops," he said softly.

Then, without more ado, he mounted the stairs, and laid his shoulder to the heavy door.

CHAPTER XXVI
JUSTICE — AND JUSTIFICATION

The court room was crowded on every side. There was barely space for another person to enter in comfort, and when the news went round in the street that Sir Nigel Merriton, late of the army, was being tried for his life, and that things were going pretty black against him, all London seemed to turn out with a morbid curiosity to hear the sentence of death passed.

Petrie, stationed at the door, spent most of his time waving a white-gloved hand, and shaking his head until he felt that it would shortly tumble off his neck and roll away upon the pavement. Mr. Narkom had given him instructions that if any one of "any importance in the affair in question" should turn up, he was to admit him, but to be adamant in every other case. And so the queue of morbid-minded women and idle men grew long and longer, and the clamour louder and louder, until the tempers of the police on guard grew very short, and the crowd was handled more and more firmly.

The effect of this began to tell. Slowly it thinned out and the people turned once more into the Strand, sauntering along with their heads half the time over their shoulders, while Petrie stood and mopped his face and wondered what had become of Mr. Cleek, or if he had turned up in one of his many *aliases*, and he hadn't recognized him.

"Like as not that's what's happened," he told himself, stuffing his thumbs into his policeman's belt and setting his feet apart. "But what gets over me is, not a sight 'ave I seen of young Dollops. And where Mr. Cleek is. … Well, that there young feller is bound to be, too. Case is drawin' to a close, I reckon, by this time. I wouldn't be in *that* young lord's shoes!"

He shook his head at the thought, and fell to considering the matter and in a most sympathetic frame of mind if the truth be told.

Half-an-hour passed, another sped by. The crowd now worried him very little, and judging from one or two folk that drifted out of the court room, with rather pale faces and set mouths, as though they had heard something that sickened them, and were going to be out of it before the end came, Petrie began to think that that end was approaching very near.

And he hadn't seen Mr. Cleek go into the place, or Dollops either! Funny thing that. In his phone message that morning, Mr. Cleek had said he would be at the court sharp at one, and it was half-past two now. Well, he was sorry the guv'nor hadn't turned up in time. He'd be disappointed, no doubt, and after all the telephoning and hunting up of directories that he himself had done personally that very morning, Mr. Cleek would be feeling rather "off it" if he turned up too late.

Petrie took a few steps up and down, and his eyes roamed the Strand leisurely. He came to a sudden halt, as a red limousine—*the* red limousine he knew so well—whirled up to the pavement's edge, stopped in front of him with a grinding of brakes, a door flashed open, and he heard the sound of a sharp order given in that one unmistakable voice. Mr. Cleek was there, followed by Dollops, close at his heels, and looking as though they had torn through hell itself to get there in time.

Petrie took a hurried step forward and swung back the big iron gate still farther.

"In time, Petrie?" Cleek asked breathlessly.

"Just about, sir. Near shave, though, from what I see of the people a-comin' out. 'Eard the case 'ad gone against Sir Nigel, sir—poor chap. 'Ere, you, Dollops—"

But Dollops was gone in his master's wake, in his arms a huge, ungainly bundle that looked like a stove-pipe wrapped up in brown paper, gone through the courtroom door, without so much as passing the time of day with an old pal. Petrie felt distinctly hurt about it, and sauntered back to his place with his smile gone, while Cleek, hurrying through the crowded court room and passing, by the sheer power of his name, the various court officials who would have stopped him, stopped only as he reached the space before the judge's bench. Already the jury were filing in, one by one, and taking their seats. The black cap lay beside Mr. Justice Grainger's spectacles, a sinister emblem, having its response in the white-faced man who stood in the dock, awaiting the verdict upon his life.

Cleek saw it all in one glance, and then spoke.

"Your Lordship," he said, addressing the judge, who looked at him with raised eyebrows, "may I address the court?" The barristers arose, scandalized at the interruption, knowing not whether advantage for prosecution or defence lay in what this man had to say. The clerk of the court stood aghast ready to order the court officers to eject the interloper who dared interrupt the course of the majestic law. All stood poised for a breathless moment, held in check by the power of the man Cleek, or by uncertainty as to the action of the judge.

A tense pause, and then the court broke the silence, "You may speak."

"Your Lordship, may it please the court," said Cleek, "I have evidence here which will save this man's life. I demand to show it to the court."

The barristers, held in check by the stern practice of the English law, which, unlike American practice does not allow counsel to becloud the issue with objection and technical argument, remained motionless. They knew Cleek, and knew that here was the crisis of the case they had presented so learnedly.

"This is an unusual occurrence, sir," at last spoke the judge, "and you are distinctly late. The jury has returned and the foreman is about to pronounce the verdict. What is it you have to say, sir?"

"Your Lordship, it is simply this." Cleek threw back his head. "The prisoner at bar—" He pointed to Merriton, who at the first sound of Cleek's voice had spun round, a sudden hope finding birth in his dull eyes, "is *innocent*! I have absolute proof. Also—" He switched round upon his heel and surveyed the court room, "I beg of your Lordship that you will immediately give orders for no person to leave this court. The instigator of the crime is before my eyes. Perhaps you do not know me, but I have been at work upon this case for some time, and am a colleague of Mr. Narkom of Scotland Yard. My name is—Cleek—Hamilton Cleek. I have your permission to continue?"

A murmur went up round the crowded court room. The judge nodded. He needed no introduction to Cleek.

"The gentlemen of the jury will be seated," declared the court, "the clerk will call Hamilton Cleek as a witness."

This formality accomplished, the judge indicated that he, himself, would question this crucial eleventh-hour witness.

"Mr. Cleek," he began, "you say this man is innocent. We will hear your story."

Cleek motioned to Dollops, who stood at the back of the court, and instantly the lad pushed his way through the crowd to his master's side, carrying the long, ungainly burden in his arms. Meanwhile, at the back of the room a commotion had occurred. The magic name of that most magical of men—Hamilton Cleek, detective—had wrought what Cleek had known it would. Someone was pushing for the door with all the strength that was in him, but already the key had turned, and Hammond, as guardian, held up his hand.

Cleek knew—but for the time said nothing—and the crowd had hidden whoever it was from the common view. He simply motioned Dollops to lay his burden upon the table, and then spoke once more.

"M' Lud," he said clearly, "may I ask a favour of the court? I should be obliged if you would call every witness in this matter here—simultaneously. Set them out in a row, if you will, but call them *now*. … Thanks."

The judge motioned to the clerk, and through the hushed silence of the court the dull voice droned out: "Anthony West, William Borkins, Lester Stark, Gustave Brellier, Miss Antoinette Brellier, Doctor Bartholomew. …" And so on through the whole list. As each name was called the owner of it came forward and stood in front of the judge's high desk.

"A most unusual proceeding, sir," said that worthy, again settling the spectacles upon his nose and frowning down at Cleek; "but, knowing who you are—"

"I appreciate your Lordship's kindness. Now then, all there?" Cleek whirled suddenly, and surveyed the strange line. "That's good. And at least every one of them is *here*. No chance of slipping away now. Now for it."

He turned back to the table with something of suppressed eagerness in his movements, and a low murmur of excitement went up round the crowded courtroom. Rapidly he tore off the wrappings from the long, snake-like bundle, and held one of the objects up to view.

"Allow me to draw your attention to this," he said, in a loud, clear voice, every note of which carried to the back of the long room. "This, as you possibly know, sir, is a piece of electric tubing made for the express purpose of conveying safely delicate electric wirings that are used for installations, so that they may not be damaged in transit from the factory to—the agent who sells them. You would like to see the wirings, I know—" For answer he whipped open the joints of one of the tubes, set it upon end, and—from inside the narrow casing came a perfect shower of golden sovereigns clattering to the floor and across the table in front of the astonished clerk's eyes.

The judge sat up suddenly and rubbed his eyes.

"God bless my soul!" he began, and then subsided into silence. The eyes of young Sir Nigel Merriton nearly leapt from their sockets with astonishment; and every man in the crowd was gaping.

Cleek laughed.

"Rather of a surprise, I must admit; isn't it?" he said, with a slight shrug of the shoulders. "And no doubt you're wondering what all this has to do with the case in hand. Well, that'll come along all in good time. Golden sovereigns, you see, carefully stacked up to fill the little tubing to its capacity—and thousands of 'em done the same, too! There's a perfect fortune down there in that factory at Saltfleet! Mr. Narkom," he turned round and surveyed the Superintendent with mirthful eyes, "what about these bank robberies now, eh? I told you something would crop up. You see it has. We've discovered the hiding-place of the gold—and the prime leader in the whole distressing affair. The rest ought to be easy." He whipped round suddenly toward the line of witnesses, letting his eyes travel over each face in turn; past Tony West's reddened countenance, past Dr. Bartholomew's pale intensity, past Borkins, standing very straight and white and frightened-looking. Then, of a sudden he leapt forward, his hand clamped down upon someone's shoulder, and his voice exclaimed triumphantly:

"And here the beauty is!"

Then, before the astonished eyes of the crowd of spectators stood Mr. Gustave Brellier, writhing and twisting in the clutch of the firm fingers and spitting forth fury in a Flemish patois that would have struck Cleek dead on the spot—if words could kill.

A sudden din arose. People pressed forward, the better to see and hear, exclaiming loudly, condemning, criticising. The judge's frail old hand brought silence at last, and Antoinette Brellier came forward from her place and clutched Cleek by the arm.

"It cannot be, Mr.—Cleek!" she said piteously. "I tell you my uncle is the best of men, truly! He could never have done this thing that you accuse him of—and—"

"And the worst of devils! That I can thoroughly endorse, my dear young lady," returned Cleek with a grim laugh. "I am sorry for you— very. But at least you will have consolation in your future husband's release. That should compensate you. Here, officer, take hold of this man. We'll get down to brass tacks now. Take hold of him, and hold him fast, for a more slippery snake never was created. All right, Sir Nigel; it is all right, lad. Sit down. This is going to be a long story, but it's got to be told. Fetch chairs for the witnesses, constable. And don't let any of 'em go—yet. I want 'em to hear this thing through."

In his quick, easy manner he seemed suddenly to have taken command of the court. And, knowing that he was Hamilton Cleek, and that Cleek would use his own methods, or none, Mr. Justice Grainger took the wisest course, and—let him alone.

When all was in readiness, Cleek settled down to the story. He was the only man left standing, a straight slim figure, full of that controlled power and energy that is so often possessed by a small but perfect machine. He bowed to the judge with something of the theatrical in his manner, and then rested one hand upon the clerk's table.

"Now, naturally, you are wanting to hear the story," he said briskly, "and I'll make it as brief as possible. But I warn you there's a good deal to be told, and afterward there'll be work for Scotland Yard, more work than perhaps they'll care about; but that is another story. To begin with, the jury, my lord, was undoubtedly, from all signs, about to convict the prisoner upon a charge of murder—a murder of which he was entirely innocent. You have heard Merriton's story. Believe me, every word of it is true—circumstantial evidence to the contrary notwithstanding.

"In the first place, Dacre Wynne was shot through the temple at the instigation of that man there," he pointed to Brellier, standing pale and still between two constables, "foully shot, as many others had been similarly done to death, because they had ventured forth across the Fens at night, and were likely to investigate this man's charming little midnight movements, further than he cared about. To creatures of his like human life is nothing compared to what it can produce. Men and women are a means to an end, and that end, the furtherance of his own wealth, his own future. The epitome of prehistoric selfishness, is it not? Club the next man that comes along, and steal from his dead body all that he has worked for. Oh, a pretty sort of a tale this is, I promise you!

"What's that, my lord? What has the Frozen Flame to do with all this? Why, the answer to that is as simple as A.B.C. The Frozen Flames, or that most natural of phenomena, marsh-gas—of which I won't weary you with an explanation—arose from that part of the Fens where the rotting vegetation was at its worst. What more natural, then, than that this human fiend should endeavour to shape even this thing to his own ends? The villagers had always been superstitious of these lights, but their notice had never been particularly called to them before the story of the Frozen Flames had been carefully spread from mouth to mouth by Brellier's tools.

"Then one man, braver than the rest, ventured forth—and never came back. The story gained credence, even with the more educated few. Another, unwilling to conform to public opinion, did likewise. And he, too, went into the great unknown. The list of Brellier's victims—supposed, of course, to be burnt up by the Frozen Flames—grew fairly lengthy in the four years that he has been using them as a screen for his underhanded work. A guard—and I've seen one of the men myself during a little midnight encounter that I had with him—went wandering over that part of the district armed with a revolver. The first sight of a stranger caused him to use his weapon. Meanwhile, behind the screen of the lights the bank robbers were bringing in their gold by motor and hiding the sacks down in a network of underground passageways that I also discovered—and traversed. They ran, by devious ways, both to a field in Saltfleet conveniently near the factory, and by another route up to the back kitchen of Merriton Towers.

"You'll admit that, when I discovered this to be the case, I felt pretty uneasy about Sir Nigel's innocence. But a still further search brought to light another passage, which ran straight into the study of Withersby Hall, occupied by the Brelliers, and was hidden under the square rug in front of the fireplace. A nice convenient little spot for our friend here to carry on his good work. Just a few words to say that he didn't want to be disturbed in his study, a locked door, a rug moved, and—there you are! He was free from all prying eyes to investigate the way things were going, and to personally supervise the hiding of the gold. While outside upon the Fens men were being killed like rats, because one or two of them chose to use their intelligence, and wanted to find out what the flames really were. They found out all right, poor devils, and their widows waited for them in vain.

"And what does he do with all this gold, you ask? Why, ship it, by using an electrical factory where he makes tubings and fittings—and a good deal of mischief, to boot. The sovereigns are hidden as you have seen, and are shipped out at night in fishing boats, loaded below

the water mark—I've helped with the loading myself, so I know—
en route for Belgium, where his equally creditable brother, Adolph,
receives the tubes and invariably ships them back as being of the
wrong gauge. Look here—" He stopped speaking for a moment and,
stepping forward, lifted up another tubing from the table, and unfastened it at one of the joints. Then he held it up for all to see.

"See that stuff in there? That's tungsten. Perhaps you don't all
know what tungsten is. Well, it's a valuable commodity that is mined
from the earth, and which is used expressly in the making of electric
lamps. Our good friend Adolph, like his brother, has the same twist
of brain. Instead of keeping the tubes, he returns them with the rather
thin excuse that they are of the wrong gauge, and fills them with this
tungsten, from the famous tungsten mines for which Belgium holds
first place in the world. And so the stuff is shipped in absolutely free
of duty, while our friend here unloads it, supplies the raw material to
one or two firms in town, trading under the name of Jonathan Brent
(you see I've got the whole facts, Brellier), and uses some himself
for this factory, which is the 'blind' for his other trading ideas. Very
clever, isn't it?"

The judge nodded.

"I thought you would agree so, my Lord. Even crime can have its
clever side, and more often than not the criminal brain is the cleverest
which the world produces.

"Where was I? Ah, yes! The shipping of the stuff to Belgium.
You see, Brellier's clever there. He knows that the sudden appearance
of all this gold at his own bank would arouse suspicions, especially
as the robberies have been so frequent, so he determines that it is
safer out of the country, and as the exchange of British gold is high,
he makes money that way. Turns his hand to everything, in fact."
He laughed. "But now we're turning our hands to *him*, and the Law
will have its toll, penny for penny, life for life. You've come to the
end of *your* resources, Brellier, when you engaged those two strange
workmen. Or, better still, your accomplice did it for you. You didn't
know they were Cleek and his man, did you? You didn't know that
on that second night after we'd worked there at the factory for you,
we investigated that secret passage in the field outside Saltfleet Road?
You didn't know that while you walked down that passage in the
darkness with your man Jim Dobbs—or 'Dirty Jim,' to give him the
sobriquet by which he is known among your employees—that we

were hidden against the wall opposite to that first little niche where the bags of sovereigns stood, and that—though I hadn't seen you—something in your voice struck a note of familiarity in my memory? You didn't know that, then? Well, perhaps it's just as well, because I might not be here now to tell this story, and to hand you over to justice."

CHAPTER XXVII
THE SOLVING OF THE RIDDLE

"For the sake of *le bon dieu*, man, cease your cruel mockery!" said Brellier, suddenly, in a husky voice, as the clerk rose to quell the interrupted flow of oratory, and the court banged his mace for quiet.

"You didn't think of the cruel mockery of God's good world, which you were helping so successfully to ruin!" continued the detective, speaking *to* the court but *at* Brellier, each word pointed as a barb, each pause more pregnant with scorn than the spoken words had been. "You didn't think of that, did you? Oh, no! You gave no thought to the ruined home and the weeping wife, the broken-hearted mother and the fatherless child. That was outside your reckoning altogether. And, if hearsay be true (and in this case I believe it is) you even went so far as to kill a defenceless woman who had been brave enough to wander out across that particular part of the Fens just to see what those flames really were. And yet,—your lordship, this man howls for mercy."

He paused a moment and passed a hand wearily over his forehead. The telling of the tale was not easy, and the expression of 'Toinette Brellier's tear-misted eyes added to the difficulty of it. But he knew he must spare no detail; in fairness to the man who stood in the dock, in fairness to the Law he served, and in whose service he had unravelled this riddle which at first had seemed so inexplicable.

Then the judge spoke.

"The court must congratulate you, Mr. Cleek," he said in his fine, metallic voice, "upon the very excellent and intricate work you have done on this case. Believe me, the Law appreciates it, and I, as one of its humble exponents, must add my admiration to the rest. Permit me, however, to ask one or two questions. In the first place, before we proceed further with the case, I should like you to give me any explanation that you can relative to the matter of what the prisoner here has told us with regard to the story of the Frozen Flame. This gentleman has said that the story goes that whenever a new victim had been claimed by the flames, that he completely vanishes, and that another flame appears in amongst its fellows. The prisoner has declared this to be true; in fact, has actually sworn upon oath, that he has seen this thing with his own eyes the night that Dacre Wynne was killed. I confess that upon hearing this, I had my strong suspicions of his veracity. Can you explain it any clearer?"

Cleek smiled a trifle whimsically, then he nodded.

"I can. Shortly after I made my discovery of the secret passage that led out upon the Fens—the entrance to it, by the way, was marked by a patch of charred grass about the size of a small round table (you remember, Dollops, I asked you if you noticed anything then?), that lifted up, if one had keen enough eyes to discover it, and revealed the trap-door beneath—Dollops and I set out on another tour of investigation. We were determined to take a sporting chance on being winged by the watchful guards and have a look round behind those flames for ourselves. We did this. It happened that we slipped the guard unobserved, having knowledge, you see, of at least part of the whole diabolical scheme, and getting within range of the flames without discovery, or, for that matter, seeing any one about, we got down on our hands and knees and dug into the earth with our penknives."

"What suggested this plan to you?"

Cleek smiled and shrugged his shoulders.

"Why, I had a theory, you see. And, like you, I wanted to find out if Merriton were telling the truth about that other light he had seen or not. This was the only way. Marsh-gas was there in plenty, though there is no heat from the tiny flames, as you know, from which fact, no doubt, our friend Brellier derived the very theatrical name for them, but the light of which Merriton spoke I took to be something bigger than that. And I had noticed, too, that here and there among the flames danced brilliant patches that seemed, well—*more* than natural. So our penknives did the trick. Dollops was digging, when something suddenly exploded, and shot up into our faces with a volume of gassy smoke. We sprang back, throwing our arms up to shield our eyes, and after the fumes had subsided returned to our task. The penknife had struck a bladder filled with gas, which, sunk into the ground, produced the larger lights, one of which Sir Nigel had seen upon the night that Wynne disappeared. Even more clever, isn't it? I wonder whose idea it originally was."

He spun round slowly upon his heel and faced the line of seated witnesses. His eyes once more travelled over the group, face to face, eye to eye, until he paused suddenly and pointed at Borkins's chalk-white countenance.

"That's the man who probably did the job," he said casually. "Brellier's right-hand man, that. With a brain that might have been used for other and better things."

The judge leaned forward upon his folded elbows, pointing his pen in Borkins's direction.

"Then you say this man is part and parcel of the scheme, Mr. Cleek?" he queried.

"I do. And a very big part, too. But, let me qualify that statement by saying that if it hadn't been for Borkins's desire for revenge upon the man he served, this whole ghastly affair would probably never have been revealed. Wynne would have vanished in the ordinary way, as Collins vanished afterward, and the superstitious horror would have gone on until there was not one person left in the village of Fetchworth who would have dared to venture an investigation of the flames. Then the work at the factory would have continued, with a possibly curtailed payroll. No need for high-handed pirates armed with revolvers *then*. That was the end the arch-fiend was working for. The end that never came."

"H'm. And may I ask how you discovered all this, before going into the case of Borkins?" put in the judge.

Cleek bowed.

"Certainly," he returned. "That is the legal right. But I can vouch for my evidence, my lord. I received it, you see, at first-hand. This man Borkins engaged both the lad Dollops and myself as new hands for the factory. We therefore had every opportunity of looking into the matter personally."

"Gawdamercy! I never did!" ejaculated Borkins, at this juncture, his face the colour of newly-baked bread. "You're a liar—that's what you are! A drorin' an innocent man into the beastly affair. I never engaged the likes of *you*!"

"Didn't you?" Cleek laughed soundlessly. "Look here. Remember the man Bill Jones, and his little pal Sammie Robinson, from Jamaica?" He writhed his features for a moment, slipped his hand into his pocket, and producing the black moustache that had been Dollops's envy and admiration, stuck it upon his upper lip, pulled out a check cap from the other pocket, drew that upon his head, and peered at Borkins under the peak of it. "What-o, matey!" he remarked in a harsh cockney voice.

"Merciful 'Eavens!" gasped out that worthy, covering his eyes with his hands, one more incredulous witness of Cleek's greatest gift. "Bill Jones it is! *Gawd!* are you a devil?"

"No, just an ordinary man, my dear friend. But you remember now, eh? Well, that does away with the need of the moustache, then." The clerk of the court, only too familiar with Cleek's disregard of legal formality, frowned at this violation of dignity and raised his mace to rap for order and possibly to reprimand Cleek for his theatrical conduct but at that moment the detective pulled off the cap and moustache as though well pleased with his performance. Cleek turned once more to the judge.

"My lord," he said serenely, "you have seen the man Bill Jones, and the impersonator of Sammie Robinson is there," he pointed to Dollops. "Well, this man Borkins—or Piggott, as he calls himself when doing his 'private work'—engaged Dollops and me, in place of two hands in the factory who had been given to too much tongue-wagging, and in consequence had met with prompt punishment, God alone knows what it was! We worked there for something just under a fortnight. Dollops, with his usual knack for making friends in the right direction, chummed up to one of the men—whom I have already named—Jim Dobbs. He finally asked him to come and help with the loading up of the boats, and gave him the chance of making a little overtime by simply keeping his mouth shut as to what went on. I managed to get on the job too, and we did it three times in that fortnight—and a jolly difficult task we found it, I don't mind saying. But I felt that evidence was necessary, and while in the employ of 'the master' we carried on many investigations. And still in his service I made this rough map of the varied turnings of the secret passage, and the places to which they led. You can get a better idea of the ground if you glance at it." He handed it up to the high desk, and paused a moment as the judge surveyed it through his spectacles. "The passage at Merriton Towers, and also at Withersby Hall—so conveniently placed near that particular part of the Fens, and therefore chosen by Brellier for his work—are both of ancient origin, dating back, I should say, to the time of the civil war.

"Whose idea it was to connect the two passages up I could not say, or when Borkins got into the pay of Brellier and played false to a family that he had served for twenty years. But the fact remains. The two passages *are* linked up, and then continued at great labour in another direction to that field which lies off the Saltfleet Road and just at the back of the factory. And thus was made a convenient little subway for the carrying on of nefarious transactions of the kind which we have discovered."

"And how did you discover that Brellier was the 'Master' in question?" put in the judge at this juncture.

"He happened to come to the factory one day while we were at work upon our machines. Someone said, 'Crickey! 'Ere's the Master! Funny for *'im* to be prowlin' round at this hour of the day—night's more to 'is likin'.' I could hardly contain myself when I saw who it was even though I had already discovered the passage to Withersby Hall. I had not yet realized that 'Jonathan Brent' and Brellier were one and the same, though I discovered that the former had a perfectly legitimate office in London in Leadenhall Street. But when I saw him I knew. After that I wasted no time. Since then we've been having a pretty scramble to get safely away without giving any clues to the other men, and to put Scotland Yard upon their track. They're down there now, and have got every man of 'em I dare swear (and I hope they are keeping my friend Black Whiskers for me to deal with). That is the cause of my lateness at the hearing of the case. You can fully understand how impossible it was to be here any earlier."

The judge nodded. "Your statement against this man Borkins—?"

"Is as strong a one as ever was made," said Cleek. "It was Borkins who—in a fit of malicious rage, no doubt—conceived the idea of interfering with his master's work to the extent of inventing the means to have Sir Nigel Merriton wrongly convicted of the murder of Dacre Wynne. You have seen the revolver, the peculiar make of which caused it to be the chief evidence in this gruesome tragedy. Here is the genuine one."

He drew the little thing from his pocket, and reaching up placed it in the judge's outstretched hand. That gentleman gave a gasp as he laid eyes upon it.

"Identical with this one, which belongs to the prisoner!" he said—almost excitedly.

"Exactly. The same colonial French make, you see. This particular one belongs, by the way, to Miss Brellier."

"*Miss Brellier!*"

Something like a thrill ran through the crowded courtroom. In the silence that followed you could have heard a pin drop.

"That is correct. She will tell you that she always kept it in an unused drawer in her secrétaire locked away with some papers. She had not looked at it for months, until the other day when she happened to examine one of those papers, and therefore went to the drawer and unlocked it. The revolver lying there drew her attention. Knowing that it was the same as the one owned by her fiance, Sir Nigel Merriton, and figuring so largely in this case, she took it out and idly examined it. One of the bullets was missing! This rather aroused her curiosity, and when I questioned her afterward about it, when the inquest was over, and she had brought it forward and shown it to the coroner, who—quite naturally—after the explanation given by Mr. Brellier, gave it back to her as having no dealings with the case, she told me that she could not *absolutely* recollect her uncle telling her that he *had* killed the dog with it. A small thing but rather important."

"And you say that this man Borkins arranged this revolver so as to point to the prisoner's guilt, Mr. Cleek?" asked the judge.

"I say that the man Dacre Wynne was actually *killed* with that identical revolver which you hold in your hand, my lord. And the construction I put upon it is this: Borkins hated his master, but the long story of that does not concern us here, and upon the night of the quarrel he was listening at the door, and, hearing how things were shaping themselves, began, as he himself has told you in his evidence, to think that there would soon be trouble between Sir Nigel and Mr. Wynne, if things went on as they had been going. Therefore, when he was told that Mr. Wynne had gone out across the Fens in a drunken rage, to investigate the meaning of the Frozen Flames, the idea entered Borkins's mind. He knew his master's revolver, had seen it slipped under his pillow more often than not of an evening when Sir Nigel went to bed. Here Borkins saw his life's opportunity of getting even. He knew, too, of Miss Brellier's revolver—*must* have known, else why should this particular instrument be used upon this particular night, in place of the usual type of revolver which Brellier's guards carried, and by which poor Collins undoubtedly met his death? So we will take it that he knew of this little instrument here, and upon hearing of Wynne's proposed investigations, he dashed to the back kitchen of the Towers—which, was rarely used by the other servants, as being, so one of them told me, 'so dark and damp that it fair gave 'em the creeps.' Therefore Borkins had his way unmolested, and it did not take him long, knowing the turnings of the underground passage—as he did from constant use—to communicate with Withersby Hall. To which guard he told his tale I do not know, but, since we have taken the whole crowd—we'll find out later. Anyway, he must have told someone else of his desire for private vengeance. And the thing worked. When poor Wynne met his death, it was at the point of a pistol which had lain unused in the secrétaire at Withersby Hall for some little time. I have not been able to find the actual spot where the body of Wynne and, later on, that of Collins was first concealed, but I have no doubt that they were brought from that spot to be discovered by us. It was very necessary for the body of Wynne to be discovered, since the bullet in his brain was fired from Miss Brellier's revolver. It was all part of the plot against Sir Nigel. How bitter was that plot is evidenced by the removal of the bodies to the place they were discovered on the Fens—no very pleasant job for any man."

Cleek whirled suddenly upon Borkins, who stood with bent head and pallid face, biting his lips and twisting his hands together, while Cleek's voice broke the perfect silence of the court. But thus taken by surprise, he lifted his head, and his mouth opened.

The judge raised his hand.

"Is this true, my man?" he demanded.

Borkins's face went an ugly purplish-red. For a moment it looked as though he were going to have an apoplectic fit.

"Yes—damn you all—yes!" he replied venomously. "That's how I did it—though Gawd alone knows how he come to find it out! But the game's up now, and it's no more use a-lyin'."

"Never a truer word spoken," returned Cleek, with a little triumphant smile. "I must admit, your Lordship, that upon that one point I was a little shaky. Borkins has irrefutably proved that my theory was correct. I must say I am indebted to him." Again the little smile looped up one corner of his face. "And I have but just a little bit more of the tale to tell, and then—I must leave the rest of it in your infinitely more capable hands.

"… The reason why I mistrusted the story of the revolver? Why, upon examination, that instrument belonging to Miss Brellier was a little too clean and well-oiled to have been out of use for a matter of five months or so. The worthy user of it had cleaned and polished it up, so as to be sure of its action, and re-oiled it. So the 'dog story' was exploded almost at its birth. The rest was easy to follow up, and knowing the position of things between Borkins and his master (from both sides, so to speak), I began to put two and two together. Borkins has, this moment, most agreeably told me that my answer to the sum is correct. But things worked in well for him, I must say. That Sir Nigel should actually fire a shot upon that very night was a stroke of pure luck for the servant who hated him. And it made his chance of fabricating the whole plot against Sir Nigel a good deal easier. Whether he would have stolen the revolver had that shot at the Frozen Flames—for which Sir Nigel has been so sorely tried—never been fired, I cannot say, but that doubtless would have been the course he would have taken. Luck favoured him upon that dreadful night—but now that luck has changed. His own action has been his undoing. If he had not given vent to this feeling of hatred that he cherished in his heart for a master who was of such different stuff of which he himself was made, the whole infernal plot might never have been revealed. And yet—who can tell?

"My lord and gentlemen of the jury, the tale is told. Justice has been done an innocent man, and the rest of its doing lies in your capable hands. I ask your permission to be seated."

His voice trailed off into silence, and across the court a murmur arose, like the hum of some giant airplane growing gradually nearer and nearer. A sort of strangled sob came from the back of Cleek's chair, and he turned his head to smile into 'Toinette's wet eyes. In their depths gratitude and sorrow were inexplicably mingled. His hand went out to her; she ran toward him from her place, and in spite of judge and jury, in spite of the order of the law, knelt down there at his side and pressed her warm lips against his hand.

CHAPTER XXVIII
"TOWARD MORNING. ..."

The flower in Cleek's buttonhole was jauntily erect, his immaculately garbed figure fitted in perfectly with every detail of the whole scene of which he was a part. He looked—and was—the exquisitely turned-out man-about-town. Only his eyes told of other things, and they, as the organs welled to the sounds of the wedding march lighted up with something that spoke of the man within rather than the man without. He turned from his position at the altar (where he was fulfilling his duties as best man to Sir Nigel Merriton) and glanced back over the curve of his shoulder to where a girl sat, bending forward in the empty pew, her face alight, her eyes, beneath the curving hat-brim, swimming with tears. ... She nodded as he saw her, and smiled, the promise of their future together curving the sweet lips into gracious, womanly lines. Behind her, on guard as usual, and gay in a gorgeous garment of black-and-white checks, white waistcoat and flaming scarlet buttonhole, sat Dollops, faithfully watching while Cleek assisted at the ceremony that was uniting two souls in one, and casting aside forever the smirch of a name that must rankle in the heart of her who had owned it in common with the man who had so nearly wrought her soul's desolation.

... Then it was all over. The organ swelled once more with its tidings of joy; upon her husband's arm 'Toinette passed down the tiny aisle, tears running down her cheeks unchecked, and mingling with the smiles that chased each other like sunbeams across her happy face. Cleek was at the porch waiting for them as they came out. He reached forth a hand to each.

"Good luck—and God bless you both," he said. "This is a fitting end, Merriton, and a new and glorious beginning."

"And every moment of it, every second of it we owe to you, Mr. Cleek," returned Sir Nigel, in a deep, happy voice. "Time alone can show our gratitude—I can't."

Cleek bowed, and his hand went out suddenly to Ailsa Lorne, who had stolen up beside him, went out and caught her hand and held it in a grip that hurt. "I know, boy. And one day in the glad future I shall call upon you—who knows?—to attend a similar ceremony on my behalf, and in which Mr. Narkom here has promised to act as best man—with Dollops to bolster him up if he should be attacked with nerves. Now be off with you and—be happy. We'll see you later at the Towers, Merriton. Good-bye to you both."

The door closed, the engine started, Dollops sprang back and they were off. The boy turned suddenly, looked at Cleek and Ailsa standing there in the sunshine of the little porch, at Mr. Narkom chuckling quietly behind them, and—remarked:

"Gawd! Dunno which is the best—weddings or funerals! Suite I don't. Yer snivels at bofe like a blinkin' fool wiv a cold in 'is 'ead. And when it comes to *your* time, Guv'nor! well, if yer don't let me myke a third at the funnymoon, I'll commit hurry-skurry on yer wery doorstep!... An' jolly good riddance ter bad rubbish, too!"

THE END

Printed in Great Britain
by Amazon